Lizzie | Dark Waters
Book One

By Suzy Carlile

Where you used to be there is a hole in the world,
which I find myself constantly walking around in the daytime,
and falling in at night.

EDNA ST. VINCENT MILLAY

This book is dedicated to Auntie Lou Ellyn Kelly.
She believed in me and Lizzie. Rest in peace dear friend.
And to Rod Carlile,
my rock and house comedian when things get a bit deadly.

Table of Contents

Prologue—Devil's Brew

He had a face that could stop your mother's grandfather clock on the spot— might never ring again. The young man looked and smelled like he hadn't seen hot water and soap in three months. Maybe longer. The smell of old beer, cigarette smoke, marijuana, and God knows what made even her gag. A pile of cigarettes had established themselves between him and his partner—male or female she couldn't tell. She/he or they, to be politically correct, had dreadlocks that had either beads or large lice crawling through them. These kids were someone's children once, maybe still were, now just temporarily lost. She imagined their mothers in absolute despair that their precious children had come to this state. That the library, where they had once perhaps checked out their first books, done story time at, now was a place to urinate behind a bush, get out of the rain, shoot up under the eaves at night with just a cell phone light to assist. Such tragedies were unfolding all over America

When she was a young reader, her home was full of books, but occasionally she went to the library with her mother and was always amazed at just how many more books she had yet to read. She would sit in the children's section, pulling out book by book, peeking inside. Like unwrapping Christmas presents, she wished she could explore them all. She learned early on that just about anything could have a story about it. These two urchins had a story too.

The homeless situation, even here in this small town, had become horrendous. The libraries were warm, had water fountains and public restrooms. So far, no one had come up with a solution, so here they were. For her, it had become a good place to hunt. She loved books and she loved reeling in predators. The library was always a good place to observe the homeless, druggies, pedophiles, and street urchins. Sad, but kids still thought the library was a safe place to study and use

1

free Internet. The librarians would watch out for them. Right? Well, maybe thirty years ago. Now the staff was lucky to just keep themselves safe, keep people from passing out in the library, or vandalizing things.

She fit in easily. Either dressed in her Eddie Bauer hiker clothes, hospital scrubs, or a twelve-year-old Catholic schoolgirl outfit. Just kidding, she really didn't do that. Today she had on jeans, a Pokémon t-shirt and blue tennis shoes. Her hair in a braid, with a baseball cap pulled down. Unusually small for a woman of twenty-seven, barely five feet tall and as they like to say, one hundred pounds soaking wet. Fair of complexion, perfect skin, a few freckles, and a small half- moon scar under her left eye. She had gotten that scar in the jungle, years ago, jumping off the wing of an airplane she'd crash-landed in the jungles of Brazil.

By the time she made eye contact with her prey, her large amber eyes and childlike demeanor had him smitten. When she got excited, there were little gold speckles in her eyes that made her look even younger and oh so wonderfully innocent. Not intentional on her part. Just an asset under the circumstances.

Speaking of prey—here he comes. He looks harmless. Pressed jeans, athletic shoes that have never seen a gym, cotton polo shirt with an ugly yellow sweater over it all. Eye contact. She will follow him back out in a few minutes.

They have met before. She had found him sitting on the bus bench across from the park watching the kids play. So typical. She said she needed to wait for the bus too. She told him how her mom ignored her, that's why she had to take the bus here. She hates her mom. He thinks she is the lonely neglected teenage girl he has been wishing for…

She had seen a photo of him, a mug shot she had pulled up from a past arrest. His wife and stepson had brought in a five-year-old girl with possible internal injuries. They said she had fallen down the stairs. The injuries said something else. That little girl was fighting for her life at OHSU. There was evidence of past injury of a sexual nature to the child that was sure to be investigated if the girl survived. The authorities might be on it now; then again, those things took time. She didn't want to give him any more time. She had done a background check. Yes, he had a past. Suspected rape and sex with a minor in another state. It never went anywhere. Charges were dropped. The kid's parents dropped it; they wanted it behind them. But this time his charges would be met. She would make sure of that.

Sitting at the bus stop he asked if she would like to meet and talk sometime. He had plenty of time. She said she could be at the library the next night; there was a secret place in the park she liked to go to, that it was magical and usually incredibly quiet. Sometimes she would smoke pot there. Did that surprise him?

No, he liked to smoke pot too, he said. Cool. That would be their first secret. Yes, she thought, pedophiles are big on secrets.

Usually, the homeless found other things to do at dusk downtown. They didn't hit the bushes until daylight. They wandered the night staying warm and alive if they could. So, there should be plenty of time for the two of them to get to know each other better.

She walked outside and headed towards the park. He followed. He had parked his car a mile away and was pretty warmed up for their little expedition. She seems to know the way. She had told him to follow her. He had to lean down a bit to get past the bushes. A thorn stuck in his yellow sweater; it poked thru and stuck him. It interrupted his thoughts, temporarily, and of how excited he was getting. She is so unassuming. She is almost within reach now.

"Come on! We're almost there."

He can hear the water rushing now. She is faster than him and the extra forty pounds he's packing is slowing him down. He trips over a few rocks and almost lands in her lap. She is standing by a big boulder, the river rumbling behind her.

He is huffing a little when he stops and he's hot, in more ways than one.

She hands him a water bottle

"Here, I haven't drunk out of it."

"Thanks," he takes several swallows.

He doesn't notice the plastic gloves on her hands in the darkening sky. She's put a little devil's brew together for him. Shouldn't be long now.

As soon as he swallows, his throat starts to close. He gasps for air, and he is getting dizzy. He tries to grab for her, but just falls to his knees and hits his head on the rock.

Is he having a heart attack? He can't feel anything now, he can't speak. He hears her say something. Did she call his real name?

"Jimmy."

"Off you go," she says, as she shoves him into the water. He is already half in.

It should feel cold, but he doesn't feel anything now. He is simply confused.

The last thing he sees is her sweet smile and those amber eyes gleaming in the twilight.

There was no struggle for Jimmy. He sank quickly. He might get caught up on a log down deep, she thought. Then maybe pop up next spring when the waters warm up his bloated body. It will be late spring before anybody sees Jimmy and his ugly yellow sweater.

She pours out the rest of the water over the rock where he hit his head. Sprays a little bleach she carries just in case. Checks the backup syringe she might have used, if needed. She goes back through the park, puts the plastic bottle in the garbage can. She doesn't litter. She is a good person after all. Her baseball cap's off now, glasses on, her hair loose, her hoody up. She puts her wet tennie's in her backpack and slips her flip-flops on. She walks home. It's dark now. She feels better. The world is safer now.

They say two persons drown every minute. 1.2 million globally a year. More men than women. You only struggle for 20-60 seconds. Death comes in 3-4 minutes. Jimmy was gone pretty darn quick. PDQ!

She may be small, but she is strong, but not for long. Devil's breath is quick, you don't want to be too far from the water. Just close enough to tip them over.

Jimmy and his ugly yellow sweater, green now in spring from the new algae, match the color of his bloated body. He is found face down along the southern shores of the lake, caught up in some branches. He had been missing since late October.

It was reported as an accidental drowning in the police report and newspaper. Looks like he passed out, hit his head on something, and fell in the water, the coroner wrote.

The wife had reported him missing after a few weeks. Police found that odd. She said he traveled a lot and didn't always check in. Mr. and Mrs. Ugly Yellow Sweater had separate bank accounts. His accounts had no activities for the last 2 weeks. It doesn't take much investigation for them to see Jimmy was not a very savory character. Maybe he just up and left for a new life. People like him do. But like a bad penny, he showed back up. This time he won't be harming anyone. Nobody seems too concerned he's dead. An accident that just happened. They had to tell the wife her husband had drowned and been here in Bolder all along. Both her husband and her little girl dead in one year. Must be horrible. So sorry.

Stuff happens every day in this world. The police file their report. Close out another missing person. They move on to the rest of the typical criminal activities in town. They work hard to keep our streets safe. With this one though, it might just "be a gift he's gone," the officer had said to the desk clerk on duty. The woman with the amber eyes would have been happy to hear that.

Chapter 1

Flowers and Rain—Cambodia 1988

John wondered if it would ever stop raining. As if waiting for Noah and his ark, it had been raining for forty days and forty nights in the Cardamom Mountains. Biblical proportions for sure if you believed in those kinds of things. John and Sarah had been working dawn to dusk, knowing the rainy season was upon them, and it was sticky hot, and beyond humid. He had started worrying about Sarah, always soaked and eight months pregnant; but not slowing down an iota. They might need a boat soon to complete things! Johns's pretty little wife looked absolutely beautiful—despite the round and drenched rat that she was now. Cookie, camp medicine woman and cook, said the twins would be coming soon and that she should be taking it a lot slower now. It was past time to get her back to the States in time for delivery, so now they had planned to get to the hospital in Phnom Penn instead.

John's pilot and best friend, Chuck Johnson, was on standby with the Helio Courier. If there was any runway left, Chuck was the man for the job. They had flown together in Vietnam and John had hired him immediately as his private pilot, officially the company chief pilot as soon as their tour was up. His family business kept him traveling a lot and Sarah's new venture required some testy arrivals and departures, usually involving jungles and challenging destinations. Sarah was determined to get her list of orchids completed before they went home to Oakland and her new thriving business, Orchid International, the soon-to-be largest orchid dealer in the world. After the babies were born, she could stay at The Lakehouse, inside her expanded greenhouse John had given her as a wedding present. Tall enough for trees, she had been able to make anyone feel like they had just entered the amazon jungle after stepping

7

just three feet inside its glass doors. With the brilliant new collection of orchids and cataloging the unusual botanicals she (and Cookie) had gathered, it would keep her busy until the girls were old enough to travel. She still had four weeks, but the rains were swelling every stream and river beyond capacity already, and John was worrying they would have to take a boat to the small runway, if the runway, indeed, wasn't already flooded. They might need a pontoon plane if this continued.

In her 32nd week, Sarah slipped on some mossy rocks while reaching for a particularly lovely little orchid, *Paphiopedilum*—a spotted, yellow, and purple beauty, an Asian Slipper. She fell into a pile of grasses and ferns and it didn't seem so bad at first. Then her water broke, and she called out to Bao, a boy John insisted shadow her everywhere, even if she had to pee, which was often! He was never more than ten feet from her. Machete in hand, ready to kill poisonous snakes, spiders, or frogs, he was also available to climb a tree to snatch a flower she shouldn't reach for. These babies were to be her first children. Sarah had been as healthy as a horse all her life, but John would not allow her out of his sight, or Bao's.

Bao yelled out, "Babies coming!"

John and Cookie came crashing through the jungle. All three helped Sarah back to the camp, with Sarah making sure Bao retrieved the orchids too. The old Khmer woman had much experience in these things; being midwife to the village women nearby for so many years, she not only delivered their babies but their children's children as well. The first girl was born in a rush. Sarah screamed like nothing John had ever heard, the rain stopped suddenly, and the sunlight broke over the child's face shining through the tall trees. The gibbons and the cuckoo birds loudly voiced their opinions too. The healthy new baby cried out loud and clear, so all knew she had arrived. Ten-year-old Bao standing by Cookie was the second one to hold the first born. Bao held onto the baby girl, cleaning her, and wrapping her as Cookie had shown him to do with other babies. John held onto Sarah's hand, wiping her brow with cold towels from one of the coolers they kept for the fauna, reminding Sarah to breathe. In another half hour a second girl was born. She was born without a sound. Not even the bugs were buzzing now. Sarah was exhausted. It had all happened so fast. John held the second baby girl, the same face, but somehow more delicate. Handing Cookie the baby, John scrambled for the radio, to get Chuck in to pick them up as soon as possible and get them to the hospital. He wanted to make sure everyone was OK. Cookie agreed with John, which was rare.

Sarah had a favorite orchid that was named after Queen Elizabeth: strong, commanding, and seemingly ready for battle. "Shall we name the first baby girl, Elizabeth, Lizzie for short?" she asked John.

"We both had outspoken great grandmothers, or someone named Elizabeth, didn't we? Marched in the right to vote in the protest back in 1930? Long history of wild women in our families!" joked John.

"1913 was the first march, John, women got the vote in 1920," Sarah rolled her eyes at him.

"And we will name the little one Lilly after the 'Asian Slipper' you were looking at when you tumbled into them! I still can't believe you made sure Bao brought it back as we were scrambling to get you to camp!" They both knew Lilly was different—the quiet one, seemingly smaller and fragile. Although Lilly was not truly smaller than Lizzie, she was most definitely quieter. They would not know more than that until they saw the doctor in Phnom Penh. For now, they both seemed healthy, alert, and hungry!

Chuck and the Helio Courier made it through the mountains, fighting the early monsoon all the way. Cambodia in June—sheet rain, never-ending rain. Sarah and John tried to keep the babies from being completely drenched before leaving for the forty-five-minute flight into Phnom Penh, all of them huddling under a thatched roof building that served as cover by the makeshift runway. Lizzie was wide awake as the engine started. The only sounds she had heard had been rain and her "jungle family". The sound of the plane made her smile. Lilly was quietly making sucking sounds, always hungry. Sarah would nurse her on the plane. John would hold Lizzie next to Sarah in the back seat.

"Bao, pack everything for shipping in the next few days. Offer still stands, if you and Cookie would like to come back to the States with us,

I will make the arrangements. Sarah and I would love to have you both with us and the girls. What do you think?" John asked. "If you don't like it there you can come back here." John and Sarah had talked about this, had suggested it to Cookie. They had all become extremely close over the season. John knew Bao loved Sarah and Sarah loved Bao. He had no family of his own. Cookie had lost hers now as well. They could all make a new life together with the twins as the glue.

Cookie looked at Bao, "We have no one left here anymore and you are like grandson to me. I know we both have memories that perhaps are best put away, and what a great opportunity? United States? What do you say? I will go if you go. Look at them, a family of drenched rats. They need us!" Both stared at the Harmens huddled together, rain dripping off their hats, mud thick on their sandals, grinning at them like the crazy folks they had come to know them as. Yes, they would go.

Bao had never been treated as well as the Harmen's had treated him and Cookie. They had given him a fair wage, as well as trained him in how to collect and package the fragile flowers to be shipped to the States. He had never been out of Cambodia. His parents and siblings had been killed when a field of land mines went off all around them. Bao was seriously injured and had almost lost his leg. The Docs Without Borders was able to save it, but he would have a slight, but barely noticeable limp for the rest of his life. With no chance of an education here in Cambodia, the Harmen's offer was a dream come true. When Bao gazed into those two baby's faces, he knew he wanted nothing but to be with them as long as they needed him.

"I will have everything packed and ready when you call, sir."

"And does that include you and Cookie, Bao?"

"Oh, yes, Sir! Oh, yes! We will most surely be ready!"

John stood in front of Bao. "I have a condition; you two must quit calling us sir and miss. We are Sarah and John."

"There will not be much room in Chuck's plane. Pack only what you need for a few days, we can get new things for you in the States when we get there," said John, somewhat apologetically. He knew Bao couldn't have much anyway but didn't want him to worry. Cookie was another story. She had her personal apothecary that she would not part with. Secretly, he was intrigued by what she had in that medicine basket of hers. Both Sarah and John had been amazed at the healings she had performed on villagers. She had kept Sarah calm with some leaves she had her sucking on. Except during the first screaming bout with Lizzie, it had been a fairly quick delivery for both girls. Having twins, in the jungle, his wife was the proverbial Jane out of the Tarzan movies! He could not help but wonder what was in Cookie's "tea leaves."

Chuck would come back two days later, load Bao, Cookie, her baskets of herbs, plants, and "tea" leaves in the back as "cargo." The remaining Harmens treasures were packed, and they all headed back to Phnom Penh to meet up with Sarah and John. The girls, all three of them, checked out well enough to travel back to the Lakehouse in Oakland, California. Sarah was sore, but Cookie had made up a salve that seemed to make things easier for her to sit. Lizzie was smiling and perky anytime she heard any kind of engine. Lilly would need looking at by specialists; she did not track quite like Lizzie. She was still a quiet baby, except when hungry. Then everyone knew she was there!

The Harmen family business, and now Orchid International, had established relations in Southeast Asia. Arrangements were made quickly for Bao and Cookie to travel with them. With the right connections and enough hard U.S. dollars, the paperwork was done lickety-split, OK, Cambodia time. Bao carried Lizzie onto the Orchid, a pink-flower-emblazoned Gulfstream jet. Sarah had Lilly in her arms. John had a heck of a time getting Cookie on board. She had never seen an airplane like this up close. In fact, the first time she had been in an airplane was yesterday, and it was a lot smaller. Still, she wasn't sure it was big enough to cross the ocean

Bao looked at Cookie and like so many times that she had said it to him, he yelled to her, "We can do this, get your fanny a- movin!"

They both grinned and climbed the stairs to the plane.

"Ready to come aboard?" announced Joy, Orchids senior flight attendant. She welcomed each by name, giving special attention to Cookie, who seemed a bit concerned about crossing to the other side of the world. "I assure you we have done this many times and Mr. Harmen has only the best pilots."

"Where is Captain Chuck?" Cookie inquired, nervously.

"We will see him again soon, Cookie, but he just likes the short flights and his puddle jumpers like the Helio Courier. Where we are headed, he would be bored to tears. No one to terrify as he uses up every inch of a runway and spot of fuel," Joy followed with a laugh.

With a stop for fuel along the way, the next day they were all in Oakland, California. After customs cleared them all, they taxied over to Orchids private hanger at the Oakland airport with the familiar big pink orchid painted on the doors. Bao and Cookie had no idea of the Harmen's wealth or connections. They only knew them in the jungle. An extraordinary situation now brought them together and they would live in an incredibly special little world of their own. A journey that had just begun. They were all home now. Bao would take care of more than anyone could ever imagine. Cookie would take over the kitchen in no time, to the staff's distress. Sarah and John had left on this orchid hunt six months ago, just the two of them, returning home with a "blended" new family of six. Although they had worked with Cookie and Bao before this trip, they had not talked about them coming back with them until one wonderful evening when Cookie had shared her and Bao's story by the fire one night. John and Sarah had looked at each other that evening across the embers and just knew they had to bring it up. They loved these two strong people. Why not ask them to come back with them? They had plenty of room at the Lakehouse and they had planned to interview someone to help with the twins. Why not these two? They already knew their loyalty without a doubt.

The Harmens lived in the family home at the foot of the Oakland Hills, called simply, The Lakehouse. It had been in the Harmen family since the turn of the century. A three-story Tudor-style mansion, built on huge granite footings, surrounded by tall ancient redwoods, was situated on a small lake with an occasional view of the San Francisco Bay, depending on the morning fog. Ten bedrooms, eight baths, a ballroom, a marble entry that Sarah filled with huge flower arrangements from her greenhouse. There was a sweeping staircase to the third-floor playroom and art studio. The library was tucked behind the staircase that you entered through tall Brazilian mahogany carved double doors. The dining hall with thirty-foot ceilings, hand-painted with plants and flowers from all over the world. The dining hall could easily seat thirty people, but everyone usually ate in the kitchen with Cookie and Bao, who found the dining room much too cold. So, Sarah mostly used it as an arboretum for her floristry design, and "office". The dining table was usually covered with vases of flowers, books open to exotic plants, drawings scattered, leaves, stems, and the occasional bugs that came in with them! Believe it or not, they used most of the thirty thousand square foot home. Near the lake, Sarah had a conservatory full of small trees, exotic plants, and thousands of orchids. When Cookie saw the "greenhouse" she felt right at home, as there were established plants already growing in there that she used in her medicinal bag of tricks. John was chomping at the bit to see where Sarah and Cookie would go with this blend of science and ancient medicine. He had hired Cookie for years on trips into Cambodia to manage the camp, but until Sarah joined him, he never realized she had an apothecary with her! What Sarah had thought were just exotic flowers, had turned out to be moderately medicinal and some exceptionally lethal!

Bao found plenty to do, helping with the girls at first, but John made sure he was enrolled in a private boys' school in Oakland immediately. John could see in Bao qualities that could be used in Orchid International with the right training. In a few more years he would be at Haas School of Business at the University of California, Berkeley, and well entrenched in assisting John where needed. Bao learned quickly, his English was perfect, and his knack for picking up other languages was astounding. John found Bao very perceptive, and he soon accompanied him to many meetings. Bao understood cultural mannerisms that neither John nor his attorneys noticed. He would save the company millions, particularly in South East Asian negotiations. He quickly became an important asset to not only John but also the company.

They all fit wonderfully together at the Lakehouse, building a new chapter in the life of the estate. Once, long ago, it was one of a pair of twin mansions built for best friends, Ben Harmen, and Joseph Riddle. They had been built on adjoining properties so they could each enjoy the small lake that lay in the middle between them. Often, late in the afternoon, they would meet at the boat house to enjoy a glass of Hennessey and discuss the business of the day. The Harmen's fortunes stayed strong, balanced wisely across the board. His friend, Riddle, not so lucky, lost it all in the crash of '29. His home across the lake burned to the ground. Some say it hadn't been an accident at all, but a suicide. The whole family was away at the time except Mr. Riddle. With all lost, they never returned, and the property was auctioned off. Now it had a dozen mini mansions on it. They now shared the lake, but not the boat house. The Harmens acquired a bit more land and the boathouse became the sole property of Lakehouse. They used it now for a couple of small sailboats, canoes, kayaks, and some jet skis.

Old money. Sarah's money was in timber, up north. John's, in railroad and shipping. Between railroads, timber, and shipping they were all taken care of quite well. Generations apart now, business is managed by accountants and attorneys mostly. Sarah and John, all that was left of their families, chose different paths—literally branching off into the orchid business and more holistic type-pharmaceuticals in the Bay Area. Now Cookie would have something to do with it too! Herbal remedies were all the rage now.

They were most passionate about plants and the environment. Like old money sometimes does, they lived quietly most of the time and without much fanfare. Home was a place to study newly acquired specimens in the arboretum, the basement laboratory, or paint them in the studio upstairs. Some plants, like people, like the light, some like the dark. Occasionally they would make a discovery in a species that was unexpected, with Cookie's help of course. When an opportunity arose to buy a floundering pharmaceutical company in Brazil, they jumped in with both feet, and all hands, one would say. Both interests would take them to the jungles of South America again, and the world.

When friends would ask why, at this point in John's life, he would branch off so dramatically, not following in his forefathers' footsteps, he would respond, "The days of timber and trains have come as far as they can right now. I want to do something different. Sarah has Orchid International, the biggest orchid supplier in the world, to look after and I have Genesis, a small but promising pharmaceutical/botanical group that could really make a difference in this world. I find it fascinating. We feel like we can pursue healing naturally and make things beautiful too." Watching Cookie and Sarah "practicing" a little jungle witchcraft, had convinced him there was more to this than he ever suspected. A perfect match indeed, orchids and medicine. Of course, it doesn't hurt having a foot in shipping either!

Wealth of their kind brought advantages and disadvantages. One could use it to help or destroy. The Harmens had never been the kind of people who took their wealth lightly. They felt it came with responsibility as well. They could have never done another thing and their wealth would care for the girls and their girls and their girls—or boys of course. But how boring would that be and what would that teach the girls? Not their style at all. They loved their work. It was all-encompassing, mentally, physically, and added beauty to the world as well. They preferred a private life when possible.

The only time Sarah opened the grounds of the Lakehouse was to raise money for one cause or another, Saving the Rainforest, the California Academy of Sciences, or the Humane Society. She was obsessed with the gardens and certain areas were strictly off-limits—truly, some of Sarah and Cookies' plants were notoriously poisonous. One recently discovered, thanks to Cookie, after one of the gardeners had almost died after trimming up one of the Devil's Trumpet vines that was highly toxic! The gardens outside were magical and after three generations of gardeners, the grounds were world-renowned. The Filoli Estate in Woodside, now run by the state and board of directors, was astounding, but it did not have the exotics that The Harmen Botanical Gardens did, nor a greenhouse like Sarah's. Probably nothing poisonous, for that matter, either.

As soon as they had returned to Oakland, Sarah knew she would stay home awhile. She was busy with the girls, but later they learned it was also because of Bao. She refused to go anywhere without him, and despite their encouragement, it took a while to make Bao comfortable with the idea of traveling. No one could convince him he would not be deported! Although the Harmens had become his legal guardians, and he held both Cambodian and US citizenship, he still worried. John and Sarah would consider traveling with Lizzie and Lilly abroad if Bao accompanied them. So, until then he went to school and when he wasn't at his studies, he was always near the girls. Cookie preferred to never get on a plane again. Life was perfectly lovely right here by the lake and as far as she was concerned, no one should ever leave Lakehouse.

But in all our lives, someone will leave, and we don't always get to pick who goes first, or how they leave us.

Chapter 2

Lilly, Age 10

Lilly and Lizzie had been playing by the boat house all morning. Sometimes they would sneak over to the gardener's shack and see what that awful old man, Gregor, was up to—a bear of a man, with a constant scowl and a growl to go with it. Neither of them was sure why their dad would have hired such a person, particularly to work in their mom's greenhouse. He had worked for the neighbors for years and although gruff, he was strong, knowledgeable, and their dad said, even more importantly, reliable. When a neighbor sold, he came looking for work at the Lakehouse. These days it was hard to find consistent, experienced gardeners, it seemed. So, if he did his job, he stayed. The girls didn't like him. Bao told them to stay away from him, but they loved to wander all over the property, and eventually, they would see him, talking to himself. Grumble, they liked to call him.

Lilly was peeking in the open window of the work shed when a black widow dropped ever so slowly in front of her face. She screeched and Grumble turned and saw her. The look on his face was so horrible Lilly fell backward tripping over a pile of broken pots. Grumble had come around the building when Lizzie yelled, "Lilly! Run!" She stood up, but too late, he was upon her, grabbing her little arms and pulling her up. Lizzie jumped in front of the tree she had been hiding behind and heard him say in that scratchy voice of his. "Little miss, you best not hang around here, there are dangerous spiders and snakes that might get you."

Lizzie rolled her eyes, no one had seen a rattle snake around here for 80 years. Snake she thought, the only thing slithering around here is Gregor. Yuck.

"Let me get that old eight-legger," growled Gregor.

Lilly had gone pale, and Lizzie thought she might just faint. The big black widow was now about to crawl under the pots when he picked it up with his gloves and held it between his gloved thumb and forefinger. Lizzie thought he might eat it the way his mouth was moving, making grumbly noises like he did, snorting and grumbling, but he tossed it on the ground and stepped hard on it. Black and red squished in the dirt, eight flat legs all that was left. Gross.

"Just in case little one, just in case. See it's dead, dead it is."

Lilly thought he was being nice. Lizzie knew he was not. He asked if they would like some tasty, sweet jelly beans.

"Come in the shed," he said to them with a sick grin.

"No thank you. Lilly! Let's go. Now!"

"Please?" Lilly pleaded with her big amber eyes.

Sweets were not something they were allowed very often, and Lilly loved jelly beans most. Lizzie saw Lilly was not going to give in, so she stepped in first, barely inside the door, ready to bolt if need be, holding Lilly's hand firmly. He brought the jar down from the shelf, opened the top, and offered them some. Lilly smiled her huge hungry smile, giggled, and took two big handfuls. Lizzie took only the black ones and only three. Lizzie liked the black ones—they tasted like licorice. Lizzie never acquired a sweet tooth. Lizzie did not like Gregor or Grumble—whatever one called him; he was bad news. She knew it. Cookie said so too.

Lizzie had repeatedly told Lilly to stay away from the boat house and the shed, especially from Grumble. Although they were twins, Lilly was slower, never questioned anyone, unlike Lizzie, who questioned everything. Lilly also had no concept of time, which caused her endless trouble. Lizzie knew that she had been born first, Lilly second and something had happened to Lilly during her birth that made her different. She always felt responsible for Lilly. Her parents and Bao had told her so many times it had nothing to do with her, but she couldn't help but wonder if fate had been different, that it would have been her that was "slower". She went to different classes than Lilly in the afternoon and already spoke several languages.

Lilly would be forever seven it seemed. Lizzie loved her so much though and preferred to spend as much time as she could with her twin sister, dressing the same and playing together as often as they could. Lilly usually only went outside when Lizzie did and was often content to stay inside with Sarah, Cookie, or Sarah's secretary Elsie. Sarah would have her nearby in the conservatory, playing with her dolls or helping mist the orchids. Lilly would quietly look at her small books in the library with Dad, Bao, or Lizzie studying nearby. They all had their desks—Lilly was no exception. This way they could all keep an eye out for her. Lizzie could wander anywhere on the property. She and Bao usually spent time in the afternoon practicing French, Spanish, or a few words of Khmer. They rarely spoke Khmer, but since Cookie and Bao did, Lizzie wanted to know what they were talking about so she had learned enough over the years that they could not slip anything by her. That afternoon Bao and Lizzie thought they would take Lilly out for a walk around the lake.

John had thought Lilly was with Sarah. Sarah thought she was with Lizzie. Lizzie thought she was with Bao or Cookie. Elsie had the day off. Lizzie had been looking at an article in National Geographic about Angkor Wat, an ancient temple in Cambodia. Bao had told her about ancient temples, kings, and queens. Someday she would go to Cambodia, where Lilly and she were born on the banks of the Tatai River. Bao told them such fantastic stories. It seemed like a place full of flowers, palaces, and a people that had big families with thousands of aunts, uncles, and cousins. They were a family of six now. Lizzie had known the truth, that Bao's family was all gone. All dead in the aftermath of war. Abandoned land mines. Mother, father, sisters, and a new baby on mama's back, all blown up crossing a rice field. Lizzie had once asked her father why Bao was with them. All he said was, "we're just lucky, I guess." Cookie told her the truth. Cookie always told her the truth, like be careful with Gregor. Lizzie read a lot—way more than most ten-year-olds and she knew Cambodia was a third-world country, still coming out of the atrocities of a recent genocide. Bao never spoke of it unless Cookie made that wonderfully spicy fish dish from Cambodia or

Sarah mentioned a rare cymbidium she dreamed of hunting someday on the Tatai river. The small, playful-looking orchids placed here and there would make him smile. There were some happy memories, yet there was a darkness occasionally. Other than that, Lizzie had never seen him show any emotion about his past. As for Lizzie, Bao had always been there. Would always be there. Cookie says it was best not to ask about the past. Lizzie wanted to understand and to understand anything she was always taught to ask questions. That would be rude in this case, her mom would say. Her dad just said some things were best left alone.

Lizzie had been lost in National Geographic for a half-hour when she looked out the window and saw Grumble Gregor going into the shack. His pants were wet to the knees and his feet looked like they were swooshing in his boots. Must have gotten something out of the lake, Lizzie thought. It was getting close to dark, and she realized she hadn't seen Lilly since lunch. Bao and she had promised to walk with Lilly. Closing the magazine, she went to look for Lilly and Bao. Lizzie felt the sun disappear behind the clouds and a chill ran down her spine. Something felt wrong.

Lilly was not in the library, conservatory, their bedroom, the kitchen, or the music room. No one had seen her since after lunch it seemed. It wasn't unusual for any of them to skip lunch or sneak a treat out of the kitchen, but not Lilly, she was always looking for a snack. Cookie had seen her last at lunch. In spring and summer, you could just walk around the grounds and graze on fruit all day, but not now, and anyway that wasn't Lilly's way. She rarely wandered outside far without one of them. She was a tuna fish sandwich, glass of milk girl anyway, every day -followed by two chocolate chip cookies.

Lilly would often play quietly with her dolls, sometimes taking them out to the gazebo if the weather was nice after the fog lifted. After searching the entire house, Lizzie went outside, careful to not run into Grumble Gregor again after the experience that morning with the black widow. Lizzie called out, making enough noise that Bao came running up the driveway.

"Have you seen Lilly?"

"No, not since this morning," he said nervously. "I will be happy to help look for her. You head over to the orchards and I'll go through the trees down the drive to the gates, then back to our secret garden. Then let's meet at the old oak tree by the lake. Ten minutes, out and back, okay?"

"Copy," replied Lizzie. They both had picked that up listening to John and Chuck talk pilot. Lizzie wondered what that really meant and would make a point of investigating. Right now, she figured it meant "yes," or "I understand."

They met back at the old oak just in time to see Grumble Gregor pull out and down the lane in his old blue Ford pickup truck. Pretty fast it seemed with gravel flying as he sped away. Although he was here most days, his nights were somewhere else. Lizzie couldn't imagine he had a wife and family. Mrs. Grumble—little evil Grumbles, she thought. Oh my.

"No Lilly," they both said at the same time. A curious thing they did often, talking at the same time, finishing each other's sentences.

"He's gone. Let's go down to the boat house and shed. I can't imagine her going there after this morning, but then again she did think Grumble was being nice with the jelly beans and all."

"Nobody in the boat house," yelled Bao. Lizzie looked in the shed that Lilly had peeked in the window of, earlier that morning. No one was in there. The jelly bean jar was knocked over and the beans spread all over the dirt floor. Probably the cat or the rats that enjoyed the gardener's company thought Lizzie.

Bao froze in the doorway, looking out through the shed and past the dock. He saw something floating. Like a large pile of leaves gathered in a swirl, it was Lilly's long auburn hair spreading out around her small head and shoulders. Her face was up, her amber eyes open to the sky, her dress dirty and torn, one red tennis shoe still on. It was her face but not her face, and no longer Lizzie's face. Her nose didn't look quite right, her mouth open. The little yellow dress, just like the one Lizzie wore, floated up higher and she could see the little underwear with the bunnies on them they had both put on this morning were gone. Lizzie could see the bruises around Lilly's neck and the scratches on her arms and legs. Lizzie's life as she knew it ended right at that moment. Bao stood in front of her, held her, then turned her hard and told her to "run to the house and get your dad, now!"

Bao jumped in the water and brought Lilly to the dock, trying to cover her up best he could. Putting his shirt over her. Bao knew Lilly would never be warm again. He also knew Lizzie might never be warm again. You don't forget these things.

Bao was ten years older than Lizzie and although she had no idea what she had seen, he had witnessed much worse in Cambodia as a child himself. He could guess what had happened to Lilly. Her clothes were a mess, her underwear gone. She was bruised and battered. He was hoping Lizzie had not seen, but she had. Someone had hurt Lilly and he had a good idea who that was. The gardener.

Gregor had a bad reputation in town and had been threatening more than once to Bao. Gregor had called him Jap kid and had made some disgusting gestures at him occasionally. Bao felt so guilty now. He should have said something to John. He would have done anything to make that last image of Lilly disappear. That look in Lizzie's eyes. But he could not. Nothing ever would.

John came running with Sarah, Lizzie, and Cookie behind. Sarah and John crumpled on the dock holding Lilly. John yelled for Bao to call the police. He could see this wasn't just a tragic drowning. He too had seen more than he wished to remember from his days in Vietnam.

The police arrived and after the crime scene was taped, they allowed them to take Lilly to the house. Sarah would not let her go, but an autopsy had to be done. Everyone was questioned about what they might have seen, where they were that day. It was thought that Gregor left last night for the city, so no one thought to ask for him. Lizzie and Bao knew differently. Bao was first to speak up and then Lizzie told them about this morning. Lizzie had seen Gregor drive away this afternoon. No one knew where to find him, but they would start the search immediately. The police were very suspicious of Bao, which only angered all of them. He was family, he would never do such a thing. Even in these times, there were still people who were distrustful of Asians and especially southeast Asians. John knew Bao had been on an errand for him all afternoon, a solid alibi. But they had all thought it was awful to see how the police had treated him.

After the police left, John had taken Sarah to her room where a doctor sedated her. She had been mumbling to herself and crying nonstop since the coroner left with Lilly. Lilly could swim, she didn't drown on her own. She had obviously been abused and murdered by someone from the bruises on her neck and body. John was in his office the rest of the night on the phone. His own people would find Gregor faster than the police. The house was dark, quiet, dead. It was summer, but a winter storm was upon them. Time seemed frozen.

Lizzie sat alone in the room that Lilly and she had shared since birth. All was the same as this morning in there; except Lilly was gone. Dead. And it was Lizzie's fault. She was so absorbed in her own world she had forgotten to check on Lilly. She failed to take care of her sister.

Bao was as close to a big brother as the girls ever had. Lizzie knew he was feeling guilty too since he had been suspicious of Gregor all along. Lizzie was full of hatred for the monster who had done this. She had cried, screamed, hit things. She had never known hate. Now it was stronger than tears. Then screams. Then pain. It was a dark thing that had embedded a seed now.

There was a light knock on the door. "Lizzie, it's me. Can I come in please?" whispered Bao.

"No! Go Away! I can't stand it!" Then she was silent. A while back he had come by her room and heard her sobbing, he could hear her gasping for air as she sobbed uncontrollably behind the door. Now as he stood here with no noise coming through, it was worse.

"Please Lizzie, we need to talk," he whispered.

Lizzie unlocked the door, her eyes swollen and red, tears staining her face, her hair stuck and tangled to the side of her head. Things tossed around the room, their porcelain dolls broken and scattered.

Bao stepped in and held her. They sat for a few minutes, looking out the window towards the boathouse. A light was down there. She stopped crying. He brushed away his own tears that were creeping out.

Bao wanted to look in the shed. Lizzie followed. He was hearing things about Gregor from the other gardeners now and was wondering just how evil the man had truly been. They went down the stairs quietly, flashlights in hand, and set off to the boat house and the shed.

"The shed first," Bao said. The investigators said not to touch anything. John had told them to stay away from the lake, the shed, and dock. There was no way that was going to happen, something was drawing them back. They crossed the crime scene tape anyway. They opened the creaky door, trying to be quiet, stepping over the spilled jelly beans. Lizzie saw an auburn lock of hair, a small red tennis shoe, and Lilly's doll. She could smell Lilly, felt like Lilly took her hand and was guiding her.

Lilly had not had this doll when they were here earlier in the day so she must have come back. For the jelly beans? No Lilly! Lizzie picked the doll up and ran out the back door to the dock. Just then Gregor walked in, inebriated. Lizzie could smell him ten feet away, drunk, staggering, his eyes beet red spider veins.

"You!" he swore, "You are dead, good and dead little spider! I killed you—but oh, another one to play with me?" He stormed towards Lizzie, stumbling drunkenly. Bao, who had been in the shadows, jumped out and pushed him off the dock. Gregor was blacked-out crazy. It was dark and the struggling Gregor was trying to find the edge. He tried to reach up to grab onto something. He was going to drown. Bao reached for a loose plank leaning against the boathouse. He gently shoved him under with it, holding him down for what seemed like forever. Lizzie just stared. She grabbed the plank from Bao and was going to hit Gregor with it. Bao took it from her. Gregor popped up one more time, groaned, and then slid under the water again, his struggling arms no longer having the strength to fight. This time Gregor sank into the dark, cold water. Lizzie just stared at his grimacing face sinking in the murky waters now. They just stood there silently, until they noticed the rain falling on them. They too were soaked now. It was the perfect summer storm. Lighting and hard rain. Bao thought, not so different than when you were born Lilly.

They put the doll in the water near Gregor. The rains washed away their steps as they returned to the house.

In the morning, the police would find Gregor floating face down and Lilly's doll floating face up, her brown doll eyes staring at the dark grey sky. The pieces were put together: the jelly beans, the doll, Gregor's history dug up with more disgusting tales than anyone could make up. He did have a family, but they wanted nothing to do with him. His wife had filed restraining orders on him and divorced him years ago after finding him in bed with their four-year-old daughter, she had said.

In a few days, both autopsies were complete. The police figured Gregor returned to the crime, fell in the lake in a drunken stupor, panicked and drowned. Another autopsy done. Intoxication, heart attack, and drowning.

The police captain and an officer came to the Lakehouse. Meeting in the library, he told the Harmen's the autopsy on Lilly showed that Lilly had been raped, sodomized, and strangled. Both victim and supposed victimizer, dead. The police considered the case closed. No one to prosecute unless the DNA came back different than Gregor's.

"Doubtful, that," the captain smirked. He shook his head.

"So sorry for your loss sir, Mrs. Harmen. I'm sure you'll want to be alone now. We will take our leave. Someone from our office will be contacting you to finish up any paperwork, later this week, after the autopsy. Please take care of yourselves. Goodbye."

He thought to offer help, counseling offered in these kinds of cases, but he was sure these folks had their own ways of dealing with things. He had just noticed the young man and girl in the window seat to the right, behind the double doors he had come through. They had been sitting there, behind him all along. Odd, no one said anything. Even stranger, he hadn't noticed them, felt them. Like shadows they seemed. Children in the mist. The twin girl?

Bao and Lizzie had been sitting in the library when the police came in. No one had said anything to them. John had not introduced them. Seems like they were forgotten, invisible. They had heard every word.

Sarah just stared and was taken to her room. John called her doctor back to the house. Bao took Lizzie's hand, squeezed it tightly, and looked sternly into her eyes. A new girl was sitting there. No tears. No smile. Just a little gleam in her amber eyes. Retribution. Good thing the captain hadn't seen her…he hoped.

Once upon a time, there were two beautiful little girls, in a perfect world, or so they thought. Now, one stands alone. Innocence, once lost, is lost forever.

Chapter 3

Trains, Planes, and Automobiles

Lilly was settled into the family plot, ancient redwoods guarding her now. Generations of Harmen's past surround her; carved angels flying on her headstone, many varieties of Asian Lady Slippers, pink and yellow petite orchids in small colored pots placed on her gravesite. She slept. Sarah and John wept. Lizzie between them, Bao holding Sarah's arm to keep her from falling.

The depraved Gregor was cremated by the state; since no one had claimed him, his ashes eventually tossed in the dumpster with all the other garbage. To John and Sarah's horror, the investigators had discovered Gregor's very sordid past. Plenty of times he had been arrested under the influence, drunk and disorderly. His ex-wife had called 911 numerous times… she was terrified of him and had refused to press charges that would hold. An elderly neighbor who never slept had seen her take the child in the middle of the night, nothing with her but a backpack. Never saw her again. Gregor had been in a drunken rage the night before and instead of calling the police this time, the neighbor figured she just departed. John hired a private investigator to learn more about Gregor. It didn't help. He blamed himself he hadn't done a background check before. He had just assumed his neighbor knew the man. Never again. Sarah couldn't look at John. She blamed him entirely.

Not one soul had anything nice to say about the man. Police seemed surprised someone had not killed the guy outside a bar, from the reports they had collected. Lizzie overheard the police saying, "Good riddance. Too bad for her twin and the family." Gregor was surely a wife beater, pedophile, murderer. Now John wondered why his friends had kept him all those years. They were all gone now. No one to ask. No one to blame, except himself. Bao had made a point of asking about him once…sorry he did not ask him why. Too busy it seemed. John swore to never be so busy to not consider his family first.

All their favorite places by the lake and gardens were haunted now. Sarah wouldn't go outside anymore—she swore she heard Lilly calling her name. She stayed in her room, medicated, hostile towards John. On good days she was in the conservatory with her orchids. John buried himself in his work. Bao and Lizzie kept to themselves. It seemed nothing bloomed anymore. All the brilliant colors faded; the sweet scents dissipated.

Lizzie had learned to speak and write Khmer fluently and thus began a secret language just for her and Bao. Neither John nor Sarah understood much Khmer if any. Bao had a Khmer dialect that confused John. When the girls were born in Cambodia, French was still spoken mostly. They had chosen French over English when they could get away with it. For Lizzie, speaking Khmer proved to be useful, many times to the disgruntlement of her parents and staff. Bao and Lizzie had become great secret keepers in oh, so many ways. Obviously, since Lilly's death, they had made a pact forever. Cookie however, had overheard the two talking in the kitchen. Before they noticed her, she had heard them talking about how awful it was here now and so haunted. Not just Lilly—her memories were happy ones—but awful Gregor really bothered them, dead or not. They wished they could go somewhere, anywhere. Although not one to gossip, Cookie repeated it to John.

John came home from a meeting in town, shouting for all to come immediately to the library, a room Lizzie had spent half her time in any way, just to be close to her dad. Bao found Sarah misting the orchids, talking to them, which was comforting to her, but increasingly strange to the rest of them, since she rarely spoke to anyone anymore. They were losing her, and everyone knew it. The flowers were the only beauty Sarah said she could see in the world anymore. She could not see Lizzie standing there. She only saw that Lilly was not. Lizzie was feeling like half of something, or worse.

They all gathered around the roaring fireplace. Despite the temperate bay area weather, neither John nor Sarah could seem to stay warm anymore. It was as if with Lilly's death they had taken on the chill of that day as well. Sarah sat in front of the fire, just staring into the flames. John stood by her chair, holding on to the high back, as close as she allowed him anymore. Sarah occasionally staring out the windows on either side of the huge fireplace. Into the trees, towards the redwoods. Bao and Lizzie sat down in the other tapestried chairs by Sarah. No one spoke. John moved away from Sarah so she could see him now, hands clasped behind him. Good grief, Lizzie thought, what now?

John spoke, "I have been asked to visit Genesis' offices in San Diego and Sao Paulo." Bao and Lizzie listened as he stalled momentarily, expecting next he would announce he would be gone for an extended time, which used to be typical since family business was scattered across the globe. Sarah continued to stare into the fire.

"So?" Lizzie looked at her dad, eyebrows up, questioning...

"I see," said Bao wondering why John hadn't talked to him already about this. Was he not included?

However, John wasn't quite done with them. "I have decided that we need a trip and I have business abroad. Your mother and I worked side by side years ago. Lizzie and Bao will learn more from traveling than they will ever learn here. History, art, language, and cultures are to be learned out there. It means more when you see the why and the where, and how things evolved. It is also time you meet some of the people who work with Genesis and Orchid, Bao. Our world is not just the four of us. This, all of this, does not happen in a vacuum!" He stammered. Now this was more like the John that Sarah once knew. A man with fire. Interest in other things, people, business. They needed to get moving on with life. Lizzie and Bao needed this too.

For the first time since Lilly died, Sarah looked at them all, like they all had suddenly appeared out of thin air. Sarah stood up, smiled a very thin smile, and said almost a full sentence, but it was directed to them and not the flowers.

"Yes, he is right, we need to go."

She had agreed. Bao and Lizzie, in shock, but ecstatic, jumped up, ran to John and Sarah, hugging them both. "Oh yes!! When?" shouted Lizzie, beyond excited to get the heck out of there.

"We will leave the day after tomorrow! I need to be in Brazil in one month, where I plan on spending some time on the ranch and on an orchid hunt, a favorite activity of your mother's—the flora is unsurpassed in Brazil. How fun will that be?" he said carefully, observing Sarah, now listening again. He smiled at her. She looked at him, making eye contact for the first time in months.

"I have the annual corporate meeting in Sao Paulo this month, but before that, I will have people to meet along the way. My goal is to take the Pullman as far as we can, leaving from Oakland tomorrow. They are preparing everything now as we speak. Then, we will fly as we need to until we can meet another train car. In Sao Paulo, we will travel by plane with Chuck, who has agreed to come along. He said he could use a change of scenery. We have not had a holiday together in so long—we will mix business with pleasure. When I was a boy, my grandparents used to travel this way often. It will be a great adventure and give me a chance to teach you about what our business has become. Lizzie, someday you will need to know all about it. Bao will be your assistant, won't you Bao?" John teased, knowing he would be using Bao for himself more often now.

Bao had never traveled with them anywhere since they all had returned with the baby girls. From now on, Bao was to be included in everything. He was family, protector to Lizzie and Johns valued assistant when not at university. He had always been there, and nothing would ever change that. Anyone who really knew the Harmen's knew how John thought of Bao. The son he would never have. To Lizzie, he was older brother, best friend, mentor, secret keeper. Lizzie never pressured Bao to tell her his story, but as she learned more about Cambodia and Vietnam, she understood that some things in this world are better left unsaid, just like her dad had warned her. Lizzie understood more the day they had killed Gregor, from the look in Bao's eyes, than she would ever need to ask. Bao knew death and not the kind of ending where someone's Grammy died of old age. Brutal killing. Necessary killing. Protect-your-family-at-all-costs killing. Lizzie may not have killed Gregor herself, however, she felt the same as Bao. It was necessary.

Neither harbored any guilt. They trusted each other's secret would be safe forever. A much-needed adventure was in store for them. New beginnings, finally.

They packed lightly, as John had promised many shopping excursions would be available as they traveled. Sarah's face lit up a little with that statement. She used to enjoy shopping with the girls. Sarah reached out for Lizzie's hand and held it. "Yes, John that will be fun. Lizzie and I are overdue for a spree." Not like Lizzie cared about clothes, but she was happy to see a spark in Sarah's eyes and feel her mother's touch again.

John chimed back in, basking in his wife's smile that he had missed for so long. "It will be fun, but also necessary as the climate changes with our adventures. The mountains will be cool at night and the canyon stifling hot all day and night. Remember the bugs are ferocious in Brazil, so a trip to REI along the way is in store. When we are in the cities, though, I do expect you all to look your best, so hit the mall! Including you, Bao. You can be fitted this evening since there will be an occasion or two for a tux. My tailor will come by tonight and fit you, sending your suits ahead to San Diego for you. We have lots to tend to before we leave. Ladies, you must have the appropriate evening wear too! You two can go out to the city tonight and find a few things? Nordstrom's, Macy's?" John winked. "We can have a late dinner and you can show off your purchases like you used to," he started to say but stopped suddenly, looking down, recalling how Sarah and the girls used to like to do that together for him. He imagined them all dancing about in their new outfits. The three girls twirling and laughing. And then remembered he had only two now. Doubtful if they would dance this time, but at least they were going shopping.

Sarah stepped in, unexpectedly, but appreciated by John. "Hurry Lizzie! Before he changes his mind! Grab a jacket, the city is always colder than here."

Lizzie and Bao couldn't sleep all night. An adventure! In Khmer, *journey,* Bao said, was *car thveu damnaer.* They were about to embark on one that would teach them much of what they would need someday. John hoped his decision would lift the cloud they all seemed to have over them. It was time for them all to have a change of place and time. Too many ghosts here right now, and Sarah was becoming a living one.

John's family had been involved in the railroad early on, mostly as investors, but specifically so they could ship timber coming out of the north. As time went on, they went into container shipping, from trains to ships. When John and Sarah started Orchid International, those containers became paramount to their success in being the biggest orchid supplier in the world. When they started Genesis, their containers were already specialized in climate control. Temperature was everything. Whether transporting alive, frozen, or dried, it had to arrive perfectly at the labs or nurseries. It seemed whatever these two touched turned to gold. Lizzie and Bao were about to find out how vast Harmen's empire spanned.

Sarah still owned several "cabins" around the country. Sarah's family had been in timber up north in Oregon and northern California. John and Sarah could have crossed paths since their parents' circles often did, but that is not how they came to meet. Lizzie hoped that on their travels, there would be time to talk about Sarah's Oregon cabin more. Sarah always seemed happy when she talked of the forests in Oregon, camping, and fishing with her family. They had a "log cabin" on Lost Horse Lake where they would spend summers throughout many of the years in her youth. Lizzie had never been there. Sarah had felt it would be too dangerous for Lilly in the woods, in the mountains, so far from home. Sarah wondered how she could have been so wrong.

The morning came and they all packed into Orchids "great white" Suburban to go to the train station. Lizzie didn't know what to expect, since she had never gone before with her dad. Their private train car, a Pullman, built in the 1920s, was a private family car in the golden age of railroading in America. Up until the 1950s, wealthy families traveled this way often. Lizzie knew airplanes had taken over and were so much faster, leaving this luxurious way of travel behind. There had been a resurgence of Pullmans being restored, used for private business meetings, family trips, and some even rented for upwards of five thousand dollars a night, her dad had told her. John had kept their train in perfect condition. He used it around the western states to have private corporate meetings and to have time alone to think. Lizzie had wondered why he would take the train to San Diego instead of the jet, and she never understood why until now. Privacy. Comfort. They were about to step back into time. When people "took time" to just enjoy the journey.

John wanted to welcome them aboard himself the first time, and bask in Lizzie's reaction, so he had asked his porter, JJ, to wait inside. They entered the back of the train, up three stairs with beautiful black wrought iron filigree railings, and it was just like she had seen in old pictures her dad had in the library; velvet and lace draperies hung in the windows, doorknobs polished a bright brass patina, oriental carpets heavy on waxed wood floors, a soft overstuffed sofa, and two high-back reading chairs set around a small black, brass-trimmed fireplace. John noticed Lizzie's interest in the fireplace. He said they used to burn coal in it, now it was gas, and it will still come in handy over the mountains. The next room was a dining room/library, then a kitchen, followed by a bath with an unexpectedly large shower with an ornate curved shower head, like a large sunflower, above it. Lizzie and Bao had never imagined such luxury on a train. John said his mother would only go if a larger shower was installed. More important than closet space, she had to concede something and so her wardrobe was limited.

There were two bedrooms. The larger bedroom belonged to John and Sarah, with a pale blue silk duvet covering a brass feather bed. The second bedroom, more of a large closet than a room, had been John's as a boy. Bunk beds, a couple of round windows for a breeze and star gazing, a desk, and a chair with a lovely little library above it. John's childhood books were about the great railroads, botany, animals, human anatomy, history, and a little of Mark Twain. Bao took the top bunk and Lizzie the bottom. The small wardrobe would be crammed with their dress clothes and their suitcases stashed under Lizzie's bed.

All Pullmans had a porter back in the day and JJ was happy to keep the tradition going. He didn't just take care of them, he took care of the train all year, making sure it was ready and usually on call for her dad when needed. JJ worked for other families that had Pullmans, but John got first pick on JJ's schedule. The porter would sleep on a bunk in the kitchen under the food pantry. He cooked and took care of all their needs. He apparently had worked on this car all his life and taken over his father's position. His name was Jeremiah, Jr. His father's name had been Jeremiah. They called him JJ, which he preferred. Sarah knew him, but neither Lizzie nor Bao had ever heard about him. Lizzie was starting to wonder about her family and how many more mysteries might unfold. She felt like she was about to begin her first true adventure. She now realized that their lives had been sheltered because of Lilly. New doors were opening. Lizzie felt a pang of guilt with that thought. She knew Lilly would have liked to look at the train, but all the noises and new faces would have confused her.

"All aboard! Coming aboard?" shouted JJ and John rang the bell! Sarah sat down on the sofa and looked quietly at John. A small smile escaped just for him and then a laugh! Lizzie and Bao went off with JJ immediately to explore every inch of their new home. It soon became apparent that every inch was well used!! Lizzie absolutely adored it.

Chapter 4

Farms and Castles

"I wonder what Lilly would have thought of the Pullman? I feel so bad she never even got to go in it, to see it. She would have liked the little bunks," she said to Bao. Lizzie felt guilty, the loss of her twin so apparent when she thought of the bunkbeds they would have shared. John could see the sadness on her face.

"Losing Lilly was horrible, and we will never ever forget her, but we must all keep living and moving forward," John had whispered to Lizzie as they settled into the Pullman, La Belle of Oakland. Bao acknowledged John with a nod. The look they shared between them spoke volumes. John had seen enough pain, while fighting in Vietnam, for a lifetime of regrets, and Bao had surely experienced enough in Cambodia growing up. Both know you must move through problems and go on, the only way to some form of peace was in action, sometimes. Sarah had basically been shanghaied and Lizzie was ready to go anywhere but the Lakehouse. The walking wounded needed to make new memories to cover the ones they all still occasionally saw in their nightmares.

John and Sarah loved agriculture, botany, anything that grew, and so of course they loved California. An amazingly prolific state growing eighty percent of all the fruits, vegetables, and flowers in the U.S. They passed apricot, peach, almond, walnuts, orange, and lemon orchards. Artichokes, greens of every kind, strawberries, and of course the garlic farms. In Watsonville, John dragged all of them off to an old Italian friend's farm where they harvested garlic. Every day they would have the most amazing meals prepared by JJ and Sarah. None, but John, had ever realized Sarah could cook, so it was fun to watch her lose herself with JJ in the small kitchen. At night they would all gather in the dining area to feast on whatever was picked fresh that day. Sarah loved it all and managed to make interesting arrangements and sculptures out of the leavings of the vegetables each day, to all their amusement. It was great to see her involved in something again. She usually accompanied them off the train to the farms they visited, but she was always excited to see what they had brought back to her on the days she "stayed in." They took great pleasure in finding her unique, and exceptionally beautiful flowers, fruits, and vegetables on those days.

When they passed near Santa Cruz, they bought her bushels of ranunculus, bright oranges, pinks, and reds. Sarah loved those the most, making them into dancing arrangements for every space she could find. They knew she was coming back to them, slowly but surely. Never the same, but like the bouquets of flowers, the bounty of the Golden State was filling her up in another way. Turned out that she and John had taken this trip long ago before Lizzie and Lilly were born. At dinner, John would cajole Sarah into sharing stories of what it was like growing up in California before the crowds and Lizzie began to see a different side of her parents' lives. Bao and Lizzie noticed a softening towards John from Sarah over the next week and by the time they reached Los Angeles, Lizzie noticed her parents were holding hands once again. A small smile began over prickly artichokes in Watsonville, a grin over the buttercup ranunculus from Santa Cruz, a giggle when the blooms off the almond trees floated into their car, and miles of grapevines waiting to ripen going through Fresno. Their love began to grow again too. Sarah bloomed out of the dark season that had surrounded them all, bringing them into spring as they continued south.

They did divert from agriculture occasionally and took a side trip to San Simeon, where John thought they would get some history in the form of architecture, ancient European design, zoology, botany, and some California 20th century fun and games. Neither Lizzie, nor Bao had been to Hearst Castle, or for that matter anything like it, ever. William Randolph Hearst, the famous publisher, had architect Julia Morgan design the castle—90,000 square feet of magic and incredible opulence from all over the world. John's grandparents used to take this train to parties at La Questa Encantada, otherwise known as The Enchanted Hill, long ago. Today it was a state historical monument, although the Hearst family still has use of it, they had told Lizzie. Lakehouse was large by most standards as far as homes go, and was considered a mansion, but this was a real castle. American royalty.

When they all came near the Neptune pool, John explained to all that he remembered his father telling him about coming here and swimming in the Neptune pool as a child. They had always lived well, but Lizzie had never seen anything like the beautiful ornately tiled pool. Bao was speechless. He understood that Angkor Wat, the ruined temples around his hometown of Siem Riep in Cambodia were at one time quite opulent. Angkor Wat had been ruins for over 800 years. Bao wondered if it was beautiful like this place once. He asked John, "Was this a temple once?"

John laughed and said, "Perhaps in his own way, Hearst had created a temple to capitalism!" Sarah had laughed at that and then just shook her head rolling her eyes. Hearst was a true collector, of many things, including women, Sarah reminded her husband. John immediately reminded her that she was all he ever needed to collect!

They had never wanted for anything, but it had never occurred to either of them to build themselves a castle or even their own home since it was always assumed they would live in Johns's family estate like all the heirs had. Sarah coveted Hearst's gardens, however. The one thing they did have in common with Hearst was they all still had their own train cars and fabulous gardens. Hearst had lost much of his fortune during that time, whereas the Harmen's had slowly but surely accumulated more. They liked investing more than spending. John's real luxury was his airplanes, Sarah's, her gardens.

Bao, Lizzie knew, at one time had nothing but the clothes on his back. Worlds collide and they are left wondering at the inequality of it all. They all agreed it was good the castle was now a museum. It was a wonderful teaching opportunity on so many levels, just like John had told them. Sarah liked the zebras that roamed the hills of the ranch still. At one time it was the world's largest private zoo. In 1937 when Hearst lost a major part of his wealth, most of the zoo was sold off, except the zebras. Lizzie, too, loved the zebras. Sarah loved to say whenever seeing a zebra, "the wonder of God's design!"

"Why would they have stripes?" John would ask.

"Camouflage, John. But perhaps because spots were already taken by the Cheetah?" Sarah would respond. That would usually spark a long conversation on Darwin's theory or whatever direction things took them. The two scientists in them loved to argue evolution. John was forever saying if we came from monkeys why are there no humans born in the zoo? Sarah would roll her eyes and change the conversation to anything else.

Thus, their mutual passion for botany and whatever uniqueness or beauty the two of them could discover near them seemed to drive John or Sarah onward. John knew Sarah's obsession, and as they went further south Lizzie could understand what this journey was about. Of course, business would be tended to, but hearts and minds were also being mended as the tracks rolled under. One bloom at a time. At the castle, the grounds had plants, trees, and flowers Hearst had brought in from all over the world. The climate of San Simeon allowed anything to thrive. Sarah came alive. She drove them all crazy sniffing out the fragrant star jasmine vines hidden in many of the secret gardens and balconies they roamed. After a full day of a special private tour John had set up, they gathered their senses, both sensory and sensible, returning like vagabonds exhausted but happy from a day filled with wonder, treasures, and shared memories. California went by, leaving them full of her past, her present, and all of them now anxious about what the future held for them. Sarah was back with them and they hadn't even hit the border! John had known what he was doing. He was gaining Sarah's trust, in the only way he knew, by showing her the world blooming again. Bao and Lizzie had shared a life-changing experience, but the day they lost Lilly, was also the day a new life began for them. Lilly was always in their plans before, where they could take her and how bad they would feel to leave her behind when they knew she wouldn't understand why. As Sarah healed, they all healed too. Some wounds lie deep, just hidden, awakened occasionally by something. But right now, they had a reprieve.

Their little band of gypsies arrived in Los Angeles, noting there were too many people, too much concrete, and too much plastic. John had been making his list of what they might need in South America: clothing, shots, medicines, and travel arrangements with Chuck for when they arrived in Sao Paulo. Some, they best take care of here in L.A. From L.A. they would take their train as far as they could, trying to reenact the trips his grandparents had taken with him as a boy. School supplies and electronics were stashed aboard. Lizzie was expected to continue her scholastics, with John in charge of math and history. Sarah— French, Science, and English grammar. Bao continued with Khmer and Asian culture, her favorite subjects. Bao was also in charge of exploration. He was unofficially assigned as her protector so that Lizzie could get out and walk daily to see the local sights, while John and Sarah managed affairs.

In Phoenix, Arizona, they would leave the La Belle. Chuck met them there with the Falcon, flying them to Mexico's northwestern state of Chihuahua, where they would board the Copper Canyon train, El Chepe. John wanted them to see the canyon, deeper than the Grand Canyon in the States. This would not be as luxurious as their train, but all the same, a lovely way to travel. The beauty of the Sierra Madres passed by homeland to the native and reclusive Tarahumara. Between Pancho Villa and the missionaries, they had good reason to be reclusive. This was Lizzie's first experience witnessing the mistreatment of indigenous people. The treatment of the Indian people in Mexico was an ongoing problem. Killed by disease, treated as cheap or trafficked laborers, they were disappearing quickly. To survive, they learned to hide. Bao and Lizzie had overheard a young man talking about his missing sister. They both understood enough Spanish to get the drift. The father, he was sure, had sold her. "There was not any food to feed her. Maybe she would survive at least with that man," he had sadly said to his friend. Lizzie would have to talk to her parents about this.

"Wasn't slavery abolished here in Mexico too?" Lizzie questioned her dad.

"Yes, it is supposed to be," answered John solemnly. "This is a different kind of slavery. They call it human trafficking these days."

"Sounds like the same thing to me," squeaked Lizzie. She wanted to know more, but then the little voice inside her whispered, no. Bao gave her the look that said they could talk about this later—this was not the place or time. She was too young to understand. Or was she?

Lizzie had seen a girl her age walking along in the village of El Fuertes. She was following a man her father's age. She could tell by the way the man touched her and spoke to her that she was not his daughter though, but perhaps his wife? Not in a kind way, like John treated Sarah, either. A chill ran down Lizzie's spine and made her think of Gregor. Bao grabbed Lizzie's arm and turned her away as the man, cruelly pushed the girl spitting the words *"vamoose la puta!"* Too late, Lizzie had heard. She understood "move along, go whore!"

The girl was just a child, like Lizzie. But then was Lizzie really a child anymore? She smelled something rotten like Gregor and she wanted to kill the man. Bao saw it in her eyes, and he hurried them back to meet John and Sarah. They needed to get on to Los Moches, to meet Chuck and the new crew, this time with the new Gulf 3 that would take them all to Mexico City and then on to Sao Paulo.

Plans change, as they often do. Bao was relieved when Sarah announced to Lizzie that her education in Brazil would begin very soon. "In Brazil, there are many beautiful, but also dangerous things you will need to learn about."

"Dangerous things everywhere, Mom." Sarah didn't hear her, but Bao did.

Ever curious, Lizzie inquired. "Like what, Mom?"

Sarah thought about something she had been warned about while traveling.

"Ah, *Brugmansia,* a beautiful and dangerous flower indeed, Angel or Devil's Trumpet, depending on how one uses it. In Brazil, they call it the zombie plant because it is known to put people in a trance, making them do things they would not normally do. People are robbed or even commit suicide under its influence. Some call it "The Devil's Breath.""

That could be particularly useful, thought Lizzie to herself. Once again, Bao noticed that glimmer in Lizzie's eyes, as her amber eyes glittered with golden speckles that she got when she found something particularly exciting or intriguing. There was also a little wicked smile she had developed. He did not know what to think of this new Lizzie and not so sure if he wanted to know.

Chapter 5

Down to Brazil

Lizzie thought Oakland was a big city, but nothing could prepare her for Sao Paulo. The bustling of cars, buses, trains, and people from all nationalities buzzing about, the smell of—well, everything you can imagine. John said, "She is the heartbeat of Brazil, the pulse of the people; a big part of our business is here now." Lizzie hoped their new home in the countryside would smell like something other than diesel.

With at least nineteen million people, yes, Sao Paulo was too much of everything for Lizzie. Thank God we are getting out of here, she thought. As soon as they had landed, they checked through customs and were immediately shuttled by Jeep to Chuck Johnson's new Cessna 208 and headed out to the "ranch"—basically a deserted, small research farm where different kinds of botanicals had been grown, tested, and processed into curious, and possibly useable pharmaceuticals by grad students ready for escape back in Johns college days. Lizzie had heard the stories about when John had worked and studied there, dabbling in the discovery of new species. John had turned out to be quite the scientist and although he could have returned early with his research thesis complete, he had fallen in love with a petite brunette working alongside him and took a "sabbatical" staying in Brazil for a few more months to make that love official. They were married to their parent's dismay, a few months later at the ranch. At that time, it was just a one-story Spanish-style, sprawling hacienda with five bedrooms and two baths, a big kitchen and a huge dining room with a Brazilian Ipe-wood table that sat fourteen in the great room. There had been a huge wrap-around covered porch, with leather and lattice chairs, and back then, of course, two outhouses, one for girls and one for boys! Their old professor, Marcus, and his wife,

Anna, had a bedroom and bath to themselves and 12 students bunked together. Ok girls in one room, boys in the other. Hard to imagine John and Sarah living like that. Lizzie never had, that was for sure! She was wary of the outhouse after being warned about killer ants, wandering spiders, and vipers. Who wouldn't be?

Sarah's eyes and smile could have lit up the darkest skies when she saw the house. John had told her he had bought it when the university let it go a few years back. It had been in bad shape and John had been having it remodeled for years as a surprise for Sarah. It took time to get anything done in the tropics especially when you had to fly into almost nonexistent runways in smaller planes, land helicopters, or truck things in on roads that had also seen better days. John had been planning this trip in a year or two, but now seemed like a good idea. The footprint of the house was enlarged a tad to add bathrooms, one for each bedroom. A huge septic system installed to everyone's delight, after seeing the outhouses. The kitchen had been remodeled, a big Wolf range brought in for cooking, an extra freezer, a huge solar-powered generator to assist with the propane one. The master bedroom acquired more closet space, a sitting area, and a claw-foot tub recently refurbished for Sarah.

John showed them around, never letting go of Sarah's hand, the two of them acting like college kids again and telling stories about when they had lived there. The old laboratory they had worked side by side in was barely still there and the huge greenhouse was a weed-infested disaster. The house had been refurbished, but they would need a machete to get through the door of the old lab and greenhouse.

Bao and Lizzie were dying to go inside what looked like the haunted house of all greenhouses! They were just about to walk through the tangles of vines in the doorway when a breeze blew by and with it, thousands of spiders that flew in all directions sending them screeching back towards the house. As much as they all loved flowers and plants, thousands of spiders were another thing! John and Sarah burst out laughing. Lizzie had never heard her laugh so hard. They all started laughing and had to sit down on the grass before they fell! John, holding Sarah's hand, said, "Remember when you saw them the first time?"

Seems this friendly little spider, *anelosimus eximus,* rains down in the thousands regularly, sometimes covering an entire small village as their webs could be lifted and carried away for miles after freaking out the inhabitants momentarily!

"Don't worry," John said, while slipping into his professor tone, "they don't bite. They live in huge colonies, like bees or ants. On one of our first outings to the jungle, I surprised your mom with a colony of fifty thousand of them with a web only about twenty-five feet long between the trees, but just the same a remarkable sight. They really are quite amazing workers. You will soon identify the poisonous critters from the friendly ones. Everything here works together in creative ways; like, if it's colorful, it is usually a warning that it's probably poisonous!"

"What eats the spiders?" Lizzie wanted to know. Always looking further down the path of the food chain.

"Bats. Thousands of bats," answered Sarah.

Just then Lizzie noticed a beautiful flower that had the biggest blooms she had ever seen. Sarah called it Angel's Trumpet and John called it Devil's Breath. It had long horn-shaped white flowers, like a trumpet, and hung down from a small bushy-looking tree.

"Zombie flower," added Lizzie, remembering suddenly what her mom had said a few days earlier.

"Why Devil's Breath?" asked Bao not sure if he really wanted to know.

John explained that the drug cartels had found a use for it amongst themselves, within their gangs, and human trafficking. It had also gotten out to the streets and occasionally shows up as the zombie drug. Turns folks into zombies and their captors can make them do anything. If their victims are lucky, they just wake up the next day robbed of their possessions, but with their lives intact—just as Lizzie was about to touch that lovely blossom too! Lizzie wanted to know more about this deadly, but lovely flower. John had made sure to tell them there were medicinal purposes for this plant that is still in use today.

"Medicines to prevent motion sickness. The local natives have used it for thousands of years to heal and to hunt game. And maybe some of the river tribes use it to keep strangers out of their territory!"

"I'd like to see how it works someday," thought Lizzie.

John and Sarah didn't notice her interest, but Bao did. He saw that glimmer in her eyes again.

John, still lecturing, said, "Tomorrow you will meet some new kids your age, Lizzie. In the morning you will check out the ranch with your mom and Bao. She will show you what to touch and what not to. Hopefully, you'll remember, right Sarah?"

"Better than you, as I recall, dear," she said with a smile.

John gave her *the look.* "There are things here that will kill you, seriously. Some move, some don't. Don't touch it unless you know what it is."

"We're not in Kansas anymore, Dorothy," said Bao and Lizzie at the same time.

They were all exhausted and settled into their rooms gratefully. The beds had big mosquito nets over them, beautiful terra-cotta tile floors, dark Brazilian hardwood doors, and shutters to keep the monkeys, squirrels, and other critters of the night out. Clean white stucco walls kept them cool along with the fans that spun slowly from the ceilings. Lizzie could see the Angel's Trumpet right outside her window. She liked to think it would protect her from evil or at the least ward it off. Lizzie knew it was the little things that got you in the jungle. She thought about the look her dad had given her mom. She had heard the stories about the spider bite that just about killed her dad. He still had the scar and obviously the memory. They had all had yellow fever vaccinations and started their malaria pills, but it seemed they were going to have to learn a lot, quickly, if they were to survive here! John and Sarah had done it. Bao was from the jungle. Lizzie reminded herself that she was born in one. She and Lilly. The jungle didn't kill Lilly. The city did. She hoped they could stay here forever.

"It reminds me of Cambodia, both lovely and mysterious. Do they have land mines here?" Bao nervously asked.

John shook his head, no, looking directly into Bao's eyes. Bao, for the first time in a while, had finally relaxed. Something he had not done since they had started on the trip. He had not been in a jungle since Lizzie and Lilly had been born and it brought on a flood of memories.

It had been a long day to get here. Luckily, John always made sure they all traveled comfortably, namely in their Gulf 3 to Sao Paulo and Chuck's new Cessna 208 to the ranch. They would only need to give the pilot a call and he would be here in an hour if anyone needed to go to Sao Paulo. The next town was a few hours away by dirt road, but the city, with hospitals and necessities, was a full day and a half by car. Lots of jungle from here to there. The roads were not safe to travel alone and the truth of it was, everything they needed was here or could be brought to them quickly. John had made sure they had anti-venom for the wandering spiders, slithering snakes, and good doses of meds for most emergencies. Owning a pharmaceutical company helped.

Lizzie wasn't sure why they called it the "ranch." More like an overgrown jungle farm. There were chickens, goats, mules, cats, and dogs. There were two large tan dogs with big black noses, named Fila and Goose, both Brazilian mastiffs. Supposedly they were here to protect the non-existent cattle. Mostly they slept and chased off monkeys and squirrels. They became Lizzie's constant partners, friends, and protectors.

The first night they ate supper with *Pao De Queijo* (cheese bread) and *Feijoada* (black bean and beef stew). There is a lot of beef in Brazil, just not on their ranch it seemed. Thus, the new freezer and generators.

The dinner news for Bao and Lizzie was that this could be their new home base for several months, perhaps years even! Lizzie would eventually go to boarding school in Sao Paulo during the week, Bao would attend the University of Sao Paulo Law School. Since John had been planning on coming sometime, the house had been redone top to bottom, but the gardens, greenhouse, and labs were still a shamble. There would be plenty for everyone to do and John would try to be here as often as possible. John and Bao would be working in Sao Paulo, often, and back at the ranch on weekends. Once the lab and greenhouses were up and going, John and Sarah had plans to press on with an idea they had years ago. In a few weeks, they would all be going on a jungle walk into the rain forests. "The real jungle," John exclaimed with joy! "Where the spiders and fauna get spectacularly colorful and ferociously large! We are always looking for new species, but also changes occurring unnaturally out there."

Lizzie showered, constantly on the lookout for spiders in any crevice. Clean and totally exhausted, she crawled under the mosquito net and fell asleep to the sounds of bugs, birds, and howler monkeys busy with their nightly chores. For the first time in a long while, she truly slept like a young girl—but never again as they say, "like a baby". Her mind understood "new species" but not so sure about what her dad meant by changes occurring unnaturally…yet.

Chapter 6

Juliana

They had all settled into their own grooves within just a few days. Amazingly so. From the time they had left home in Oakland to setting foot at the ranch, nothing had been routine. There had been a new town every day, new faces and places to see. Trains, planes, and bumpy road jeeps.

John's ancient "Willy" was another story. It was a Jeep, mom said, that could and would go anywhere, or so the boys thought. The problem was it was tough to get parts and often they used the Range Rover. But John did love him. Willy was a "him," Lizzie figured because her dad wouldn't dare swear at a "her" like that. "Friggin Willy! Died the other side of the ranch again. Walked back. Such a dick!" he swore. Sarah would just toss the keys to the Rover at him, smiling. They found that Sarah rarely went anywhere anyway, plenty to do here. Turned out she was the one who really wanted to stay. Plants and flowers to rediscover all the time. Sarah would be so absorbed she wouldn't hear anything, even Chuck's crazy plane dive-bombing the house.

John had bought a Cessna 208 Caravan to shuttle them around Brazil. He couldn't fly it yet—and he made a point of flying all their planes, but his old pilot friend, Chuck Johnson, now based in Sao Paulo, was more than happy to take it on. Chuck had traveled here when Sarah and John were here. He had flown charters all these years, just a little work for John in the beginning, but now almost full-time for John and Orchid International. Chuck's Skymaster was ancient, beautiful, and still had tons of great stories left in her. But too old for John's girls. John had sent Chuck to train in the Cessna 208, and he was there in Sao Paulo waiting for them with the new Caravan. Sarah was ecstatic to see that new plane. Plenty of room for all their stuff, plus supplies and iceboxes for specimens to travel.

Lizzie would learn to fly all their planes someday, but she really loved that old "Push me, pull me" Skymaster of Chuck's, too. They called her his "mistress." According to John, it would be cheaper to get a real mistress instead of that plane. Lizzie's first plane was a Piper Super Cub, and she flew it before she ever hit a paved road in the Rover. Bao taught her to drive the Range Rover that summer on the ranch. Sarah, wouldn't let them take the Willy, being that—well, it friggin broke down most of the time.

Lizzie's tenth and eleventh years were truly formidable. Her twin sister killed; she had been involved in a murder. She left the only home she had ever known and moved to the jungle. She learned to fly and then drive. She still didn't like spiders or snakes, which to her dismay were everywhere. She learned to always shake your shoes out and never leave your screens open.

The ranch had an indigenous family who claimed they had lived on this land forever. The Spanish, then the Portuguese stole it, many of the indigenous peoples, gifted with diseases unknown to them, had died off or were killed when they would not work for the new white devils. The foreigners had come and gone, the jungle too hard for them or what they searched for not forthcoming. Hundreds of years past, a mixture of cultures, blended, had learned to work together, although the land still was owned by foreigners. John hired some local tribesmen and boys to take care of the grounds and the animals. Their women and girls took care of the kitchen, garden, and house. Sarah needed help with Lizzie when she was home from school, and Fernanda, the housekeeper, knew a girl, Juliana, who spoke English, Portuguese, and Spanish who could help them out.

Juliana had learned to write and speak these languages while at a Catholic mission that had taken her in. An old woman had just left her, one deluge of day, on the church steps, dirty, wet, hair matted, and clothes two sizes too big. She thought she was ten then. She was too old now at sixteen to stay at the mission. That day would be the first day in her life, that Juliana had a real bath in a tub, new clothes, and a bed of her own. She really had no idea when her real birthdate was, but she counted that day forward as the day. These were the first real presents she had ever been given. A room of her own, new clothes, and a small wage. Lizzie was excited to have her as an older "sister," teacher, and friend. They would be gifts to each other forever now.

It was good to have Juliana as Bao was starting to spend more time now with John, in the jungle, and on trips into Sao Paulo. Lizzie did not know then, but John was sharing everything with Bao about Orchid International: how they hunted, harvested, shipped, and managed it all. Genesis Pharmaceuticals and Botanicals were exploding in Brazil and that was John's first passion. They would spend more time together here, for the next five years, than in the States. Sarah would not go back until Lizzie left for college. She would say those were some of the best years of her life, a simple life here at the ranch, summers, and holidays with Lizzie and Bao. She would sometimes stare off, and they all would know she was thinking about Lilly. They knew someday they would return home to Oakland when Sarah's demons had settled.

In the meantime, Lizzie developed a quick friendship with Juliana. She taught her Portuguese and Spanish. Lizzie mastered both quickly. They talked about the things young girls wondered about. Sarah was not capable of talking with Lizzie about "private" things. Sarah could talk about orchids and bugs and bees, but not the birds and the bees. Perhaps she thought Juliana would be a better one to share the more sexual side of life than she. Sarah had never spoken of what had happened to Lilly, but Lizzie knew all too well. She really didn't want to talk about "it" anyway.

Juliana had been raised by nuns, basically, and had about as odd a view of sexuality as Lizzie did. The animals on the ranch gave them the basics. Her parents were affectionate. That's all she needed to know. However, as girls do, they shared secrets in the dark, scary nights sometimes. Lizzie shared with Juliana what had happened to Lilly, and about Gregor's fortunate demise. Not in detail of course! She would never forget the cloud that came over Juliana, like she had a memory, but wasn't sure it was hers. She started to cry, which Lizzie had never seen her do before. Juliana shared that the same happens to many girls and boys here in Brazil. Her little sister and brother were taken by "traffickers" or most likely sold to some other lecherous men as farmworkers. The nuns said she had been left at the church to save her life, they were sure. God is great they would say. He has saved us. Lizzie did not pray. Juliana believed in this Jesus. Where was he when Lilly and Juliana's siblings needed him, wondered Lizzie? Lizzie knew what happened to her sister. She had overheard the police talking in her dad's office that night. Lilly had been raped, sodomized, she had been strangled. Lizzie looked those words up in the library that day. Listening to Juliana she understood that this was a wicked, brutal fact of mankind in all the world. Not just in her own backyard. She would not let this happen to them no matter what, and Lizzie knew what "no matter what" meant, didn't she?' She remembered Gregor's suffocating bulbous red face going under one last time. She smiled. Juliana thought it odd to see Lizzie smile just then.

Even though Lizzie did not believe in God, Juliana and she made their own pact of loyalty like the local kids did. They shared their most private stories and swore in blood by cutting their pinky fingers, entwining them in the blood that bound them forever. In the next few years, Lizzie would witness the disappearance of village children way too often. Not that they went to town that much, but when they did, she was quick to say hello to familiar faces. When she was in boarding school in Sao Paulo, she got to know some of the working children in the plaza where they shopped and ate during parent weekends. A year had passed when they came to that plaza to shop and eat. Juliana asked what had happened to the two girls who had worked at the pizzeria. The old man shrugged and said, "They ran off, how would I know?" He raised an eyebrow and laughed with the other men around the table.

Two years later Lizzie saw one of the girls on the sidewalk. She hardly recognized her. In two years, she had aged ten. Lizzie overheard the girl ask if Bao would like some sex—"good deal for you, anything you want, maybe do some cocaine, heroin?"

Lizzie stepped up "Luanna, don't you remember me?"

Luanna looked surprised "Lizzie, Juliana, Bao?!" Now she looked embarrassed.

The girl they once knew was there behind the drowsy-looking big brown eyes. She was skin and bones. Starving, now that they really looked at her.

"Please let us buy you something to eat and chat a minute." Asked Lizzie.

Launa looked around, nodded, and agreed. She was so very hungry. "We could go around the corner. That way they can't see us, but if the men yell, I can run right back. Just you and Juliana, not Bao."

"What men?"

"You don't want to know."

They sat and bought a pizza, watching Luanna eat. Lizzie asked Luanna what was happening, that the man at the café had said she had run away. "No," she said quietly, "he sold us. My sister Juanita is dead. She fought them. They made her take so many drugs and she became addicted to heroin and cocaine. I found her dead in the back alley behind a dumpster. They just threw her out, like garbage, when they were done with her. The *policia* say it was just another overdose, but they killed her all the same. Carlos needed more money and he sold her to a local gang. Yes, she did drugs. We have to. You can't bear it otherwise." Tears were streaming down her face. The man came in and grabbed her arm, pulling her away from the table. Lizzie noticed the infected needle marks behind her legs as he yanked her away from the table.

"Who is this?" snarled the man with a red scar running down his face, looking hungrily at Lizzie. Just then Juliana came back from paying the bill. The look on both ladies' faces intimidated even him. Bao stepped inside the doorway. Outnumbered, the man decided it best to take his girl and go hustle elsewhere. Juliana sat down. She held Lizzie's shoulder down, keeping her seated as she looked as if she was going to bolt after them. Everyone was staring at them. Carlos and Luanna had disappeared into the chaotic crowds of the Sau Paulo streets.

The look in Lizzie's eyes told Juliana everything. Lizzie wanted to go after them, save the girl, kill the man. She had seen this look in women who never returned. Mothers who went after their daughters sometimes to never return themselves.

Years later Lizzie would come back to Sao Paulo to work in a free medical clinic. Nothing had changed—if anything it was worse. Human and sex trafficking in Brazil is only second to Thailand. Brazilian women are sold and sent to countries all over the world. One thing she knew—once they were taken, they were never seen again. Lizzie never saw or heard of Luanna again. Juliana, in a way only she could say to Lizzie. "Life is not fair. Life is sometimes brutal here in Brazil. We will make our way the best we can, and if we are lucky, maybe we can help make a difference someday. Today we must pray to God for her and those like her."

Lizzie was not sure what she would do or when, but she would make a change. Juliana had her ways, Lizzie would have her own. Prayer was not in her plans. She would leave that up to Juliana. It couldn't hurt, but it wasn't going to be enough. Not for Lizzie.

Chapter 7

The Education of Lizzie

They stayed in Brazil for five fruitful years. Lizzie occasionally went with John and Bao up north to the Lakehouse in Oakland. Her mom was happy here on the ranch and there seemed to be plenty for her to do with managing the ranch, collecting, and cataloging new species of orchids, plants, and the occasional insect that people dropped off, while of course keeping an eye out for Lizzie and Juliana when they were home.

Between Juliana, Sarah, John, and Bao, Lizzie managed to learn several languages and cultures. True, because of Bao, Lizzie probably knew more about Southeast Asia than anyone in their family, other than Bao and Chuck. Between her mom and dad—math, science, and history were well covered. Juliana was a perfectionist in languages and grammar. The nuns had taught her well. At fifteen, Lizzie's dad had her doing the orders for the ranch. Sarah would give her a shopping list for the laboratory: microscopes, test tubes, beakers, Bunsen burners, Petri dishes, slides, etc. Lizzie always knew where to get a good deal through Genesis's connections or a local supplier. She had done so well in her science classes at school, the teacher even deferred to her on occasion. Sometimes Juliana or Bao might have to do the actual negotiating, since Lizzie was still too young to legally sign a contract. And Lizzie looked twelve even though she was now sixteen. Occasionally Sarah would have a use for a controlled substance or a "plant" that only Bao could acquire from the tribe. By the time Lizzie was 16, she was quite aware of the darker side of Brazil and what people would sell to survive. Not just drugs, either. Her curiosity, stubborn disposition, and Bao's inability to say no to her got them into a few undesirable, if not dangerous, situations.

In Sao Paulo, Lizzie had almost been kidnapped. Not unusual in Brazil. Particularly people from wealthy families were targeted. Two men started to grab her and were about to push her into a waiting car. Bao and she had been separated for just a few minutes. Lizzie had gone into a jewelry store to buy Sarah something for Christmas and Bao had gone to a leather shop next door to get something for John. He must have sensed something was wrong and turned back just in time to see a man dragging Lizzie towards a shadowy-looking black sedan. Another man had the car door open ready to push her in. Next thing Lizzie knew, the man was down on the sidewalk then struggling to stand up. He hobbled over to the car holding his side, got in, and it sped away before anyone could even yell for help. Bao pushed Lizzie back into the jewelry shop. But not before she noticed blood on the sidewalk. Was Bao hurt? No. Had Bao stabbed him? Shot him? She hadn't heard anything. Bao had always sworn to keep her safe. Most likely they were looking for ransom money. On the darker side, who knows where Lizzie may have ended up. She wondered how they knew to grab her today. Was it random, grab and go just outside an exclusive jewelry shop? Where were the usual guards the business typically had? Most likely an inside job thought Bao.

Bao told John what had happened, but they chose not to tell Sarah. Since Lilly, nothing was ever said to Sarah that might upset her. It had taken a long time for her to quit talking to plants and to reconnect with people again as it was. This incident was enough to push John's decision that it was time for them all to go back to Oakland. Sarah agreed it was time for her daughter to learn how to live in the "real world," and they all would return to the States in time for Lizzie to prepare for university. She was sure she wanted to work in medicine but didn't want to be tied down to thirteen years of school. She wanted to see the world.

Lizzie took the entry exams to San Francisco State University and passed with flying colors. She would major in nursing with minors in biology and botany. For all practical purposes, Lizzie was already a biologist and a botanist. She had grown up working alongside the best—Sarah and John in their laboratory and nurseries at the ranch.

Lizzie had quickly identified plants and tested their compounds, along the way discovering some interesting characteristics in some of them. She took a particular interest in studying the "poisonous" or "medicinal" plants with cyanogenic possibilities the locals shared with her.

She had typed Sarah's papers for articles that were getting published in botany and herbalist journals. Sarah had become much respected in holistic medicine circles, and her works had been used, occasionally, in double-blind studies. Genesis Pharmaceuticals was beginning to use more organic formulations as society turned away from drugs more often when the side effects were starting to outweigh the benefits.

Lizzie didn't want to work in a lab totally, she enjoyed working with people, interacting, hearing fresh ideas. Lizzie wanted to help heal. She had seen a lot of illness in Brazil, so much of it preventable. Since she also had spent most of her life in only two places, both sheltered, she was very anxious to see more of the world. After five years at the University of San Francisco, she graduated at the top of her class, *summa cum laude*, with degrees in all three, nursing, biology, and botany. Lizzie would travel to Africa, Cambodia, Guatemala, and eventually back to Brazil with a group of health professionals associated loosely with the World Health Organization. For three years she would work in villages at mobile health clinics using whatever she had been able to collect, beg, or borrow from connections back in the States. Her mom and dad were proud of her, but Sarah was sure she would get some disease, like Ebola, and never return. John, bless the scientist in him, always managed to ask in fine detail what she had seen that was working and the truth about what was not. They both always asked if she learned any "Cookie medicine" from the locals. Life was a far cry from the Lakehouse, closer to the ranch house, and more like some of the camping trips in the jungle with Chuck, Bao, and John while in Brazil. Most of the time they had running water, an outhouse, and great mosquito nets over their beds. Lizzie enjoyed the camaraderie but didn't let anyone get too close. She liked to tell herself they would look at her differently if they knew where she came from. If she was able to help supply something, it was always "mums, the word" to whoever was in command. Most of the docs and med staff were here to pay off student loans or had grants, a few had run away from family, and who knows, maybe one like, her just keeping their secrets at bay. They were generally too tired at the end of the day to talk about much other than what was happening there at the hospital. The work was hard and often unforgiving. Some of the interns drank, smoked pot, or indulged in serial romances. Lizzie managed to always work herself so hard that exhaustion eliminated those potential habits. They all just accepted each other. Well, mostly. There were always a few snoops she had to sidestep.

Between missions and at holidays if she could, she would make her way back home—sometimes Brazil, sometimes Oakland. Her mom, dad, and Bao meant home to her, wherever they were. Juliana had married. Her husband worked for John and they lived in Sao Paulo. Juliana had started a safe house for children and girls who somehow had been able to escape from the sex/human traffickers. She had never forgotten what had happened to the two girls at the pizzeria, almost to her, and of course to Lilly. They never told Lizzie's parents about Luanna or Juanita. Lizzie wondered if everyone kept so many secrets.

Lizzie had made a good friend with an amazing American woman while working at a mobile clinic in Arusha, Tanzania. Kathryn worked with an organization that was helping albino people find housing, healthcare, education, and jobs. The albino children were hunted for body parts and considered magical, but taboo to be close to. They needed as much help as the organization could give them. No one would come to the clinic when the albinos came in, so Lizzie went to them. Albino limbs and organs sell in the tens of thousands, supposedly bringing good luck, but Lizzie guessed being near a "live albino" was not so lucky? She had volunteered to come to Kathryn's albino clinic and do whatever she could to treat them. They provided vaccinations, birth control, basic medical care, and education against skin cancer. Skin cancer was the number one killer for albinos, next to being sold for body parts. Access to glasses to protect their eyes, long sleeve shirts, hats, sunscreen, all were needed for basic survival.

Being raised in Brazil, Lizzie had seen a lot of prejudice against indigenous peoples from the blended masses of Brazil. Everywhere she had gone she had witnessed plenty of racism, but never to the extent of the albinos of Africa. She was amazed at what Kathryn was trying to accomplish. Kathryn, like Juliana, had received many anonymous death threats over the years. Lizzie was overwhelmed with the unfairness of this world and its injustices, whether in Africa, South America, or her own homeland. Lizzie stayed with Kathryn for as long as she could, taking two rounds of tour at the clinic. She begged whatever Genesis Pharmaceuticals could supply. Kathryn was suspicious of Lizzie's connection to the pharmaceutical company, but she had learned in Africa early on not to ask questions, just say thank you. Maybe because she never asked, Lizzie felt she could trust her.

Lizzie would have stayed there with Kathryn forever. She loved Arusha, most of her people, the elephants, and OMG, the coffee. Oh yes, she so loved the coffee. On one fine, sunny, aroma-filled, coffee-bean-roasting Arusha day, Bao called. "Juliana is missing. You must return right away to Sao Paulo. The jet will be at the airport for you in hours. Joy will let you know when they are arriving. Get your things in order quick, she has been kidnapped, Lizzie. We need you here."

Lizzie ended the connection on her pink iPhone, a luxury her mother insisted that she carry. Kathryn saw the terror on Lizzie's face. That night over their last dinner together, Lizzie told her everything; about her parents, Orchid International, Genesis, Juliana, who Bao was, things she had never shared with her associates. In the morning Kathryn helped her pack her bulging backpack stuffed with Arusha coffee, brought her a mug to go, then took her to the airport herself in her rattle trap, barely beige anymore, Land Rover.

There were a few private jets on the tarmac, some safari outfits, but only one Gulf 3 with a pink orchid on it. Left eyebrow up, Kathryn who knew how Lizzie loved orchids and now about Orchid International, smiled and said, "Your ride?" Lizzie didn't need to say anything. Lizzie hugged her and wished her well until they met again. "*Hakuna matata*, my dear friend. All will be well." Kathryn hugged her and let her go. The Orchids chief pilot, Pete, waited impatiently while she was rushed through customs, then he hugged her, and they ran to the plane.

Pete had known Lizzie since she was ten. The person he saw before him was a grown woman now and ready for battle. They had barely taxied in, parked, and refueled while flight plans and customs were checked over again. Hard U.S. dollars exchanged, and they were on their way. There was no idle chatter today. No questions of anyone.

Bao called and checked that Lizzie was on the jet and assured her that they would find Juliana.

"We have a lead," and then he added, "They also have the twins."

Lizzie wished he wouldn't have told her that. Her mind raced in a thousand directions. They were just little girls. She knew Juliana could handle anything. Would do anything to protect them. It would take an Ambien and an exceedingly rare for Lizzie, glass of her dad's Macallan 12-year-old single malt whiskey to even start to calm her raging brain. Somewhere over the Atlantic Lizzie dreamed an old nightmare of dark waters and then her dream turned into one with Juliana lost at sea, the girls holding onto a grey capsized raft as waves crashed over them all. They were sinking, their faces and hair spread out all around them. Shadows of sharks, circling their teeth gnashing....

Chapter 8

What Goes Up, Eventually Comes Down

A few hours out from Sao Paulo, Lizzie woke up. Just awakening—she wasn't quite sure where she was—the hum of the engines changed slightly as Captain Pete Jensen and co-pilot Rick Mahon started their slow descent into Brazil and the pitch roused her a bit. Lizzie usually slept well on planes, but she'd needed the Ambien. She should have skipped the scotch. Her mouth was bone dry. Her head full of its own weather patterns, clearing from hurricanes to strong winds.

She had found the Ambien in the bathroom. Her mom still used it after all these years. Sarah still had nightmares sometimes. Maybe Lizzie didn't have them so much because Bao and she had killed off their demon. Another seems to have appeared now. She used to have nightmares with little girls' bodies afloat, one red shoe on a foot. Sometimes the dream had a blue shoe. Her shoe. Lilly always had red tennis shoes and Lizzie blue. They were one-half size different. Lizzie, bigger and always stronger, but not funnier. Lilly was the funnier half. Lizzie could use one of Lilly's silly knock-knock jokes about now. Strange the things we remember at a time like this.

Fourteen hours out, Lizzie was famished! Joy, their most loyal crew member, was headed towards her with a bottle of Perrier, with lime and some sandwiches. She always knew what Lizzie loved. Slices of fresh mango and strawberries, turkey sandwiches on French bread with avocado. How they got it all together so fast she never could figure out. Maybe that's why they had all been with the Harmen's for so long. Joy, Rick, and Pete had been the family's main flight crew back when they left Oakland. John traveled a lot and had another six corporate pilots for the Gulf 3 and the Falcon. Chuck took care of the Cessna 208,

Lizzie's Piper Super Cub, and eventually the Stearman now. He could fly anything, and he did, but he liked the small aircraft. Lizzie loved Chuck like an uncle, they were two birds of a kind. In more ways than either of them knew.

Lizzie knew her dad flew with him in Vietnam and Cambodia. Chuck was the one who flew the twins out in the Helio Courier to Phnom Penh. Lizzie wasn't sure what he was doing there, and John said it was best not to ask, but he had shared stories with Lizzie. After all, they spent a lot of time in the air teaching her how to fly and working on planes. Chuck was happy here in Sao Paulo and at the ranch. He never talked about his own family, so she assumed he didn't have one. The Harmen's were it; he would say when asked. Like Bao, Lizzie generally could talk him into anything if she really tried. Chuck and Lizzie took those planes places John might not have been real keen on, but Lizzie learned to land just about anywhere. They were able to get things for Sarah they wouldn't have been able to get any other way. Sarah's happiness was always at the forefront. "Mama's happy, everyone's happy," John and Chuck would say. Such corn dogs.

Sure, it was true Lizzie had kind of crashed her Super Cub early in her flying career. She lost power on take-off and had to land it between a couple of bushes at the end of the field to keep from running head-on into an ancient Shiringa tree (amazon rubber tree). She just sheared the wings off, but Lizzie was fine. Plane totaled. No explosion. A miracle. Sarah was terrified and wouldn't let her fly again for a while. So, Lizzie started to drive. All agreed after a few weeks of her driving with multiple mishaps, including taking out the greenhouse doors in reverse, that maybe the air was a safer bet for Lizzie for now, let alone everyone else. For her 16th birthday, her dad bought her a 1942 Boeing Stearman biplane. This was like going from a Volkswagen to the Rolls Royce of biplanes. Lizzie could fly the distance to Sao Paulo, but no further, and land almost anywhere. She didn't know where they had found it, but Chuck did a great job. It had a blue fuselage and yellow wings that glimmered when Lizzie would pass over the ranch, rocking her wings and waving her arms, like Amelia Earhart come home. Lizzie called it a •

"he" since "he" was the closest thing she had to a boyfriend or for that matter wanted. And she was madly in love with that Stearman.

She never really wanted much to do with boys or for that matter other children. It's not like Lizzie hung out with kids her own age, watched TV, or read romance novels. Her parents were nerds. She was surrounded by grownups. She was a nerd too, with delusions of being Amelia Earhart or Beryl Markham. Although Beryl was much racier than Lizzie could imagine or knew. It was the daring—the endless curiosity of what was over the next mountain that kept Lizzie flying. The focus, the freedom, the thrill sometimes that she wouldn't make it. But she never told anyone that. She felt so alive when she had problems to solve. Right now, she had Juliana and the twins to find and to deal with whoever had abducted them.

She continued to reminisce: when this was settled, she would go for a flight in the Stearman. It had been a long time. Shake it all off with a few rolls, loops, and hammerheads. Maybe take the girls!

She went back to thinking about her friend and teacher. Juliana had met Jake at the ranch one winter. That was the first time Lizzie really thought about men in that way. Lizzie saw how they looked at each other. John noticed too and suggested Lizzie give them some privacy. "Let them talk," he whispered, "They could use a little alone time you know!"

Lizzie liked Jake a lot, so it was okay she guessed. John didn't usually bring business to the ranch, but he had asked Sarah if Jake could come out for a long weekend of R & R. He had really admired his work and wanted to get to know him more on a personal level. Lizzie knew John had spoken highly of Jake and how he managed the Sao Paulo offices ethically, and profitably, two things that didn't go together in South America often. Pharmaceuticals were big in Brazil, and Jake had been vice president for Orchid International in Brazil prior to coming on board with Genesis. Anyway, John needed time with the family, and he wanted time with Jake. Later Lizzie realized both her mom and dad had thought Juliana and Jake might be a good match. So why not throw caution to the wind and have a little fun holiday with two of their favorite people…

Turns out Jake knew a lot about airplanes too. After seriously vetting him, Chuck let him take Juliana out in the new Super Cub. Chuck thought they needed to have one on hand just in case they had need of some short take-off and landings. And the Super Cub was fun. Nobody but Lizzie or Chuck flew the Stearman. John and Lizzie took the bi-plane and they toured about showing Jake the countryside and some gorgeous waterfalls upriver. They also flew over some small settlements, with Juliana pointing out where she thought she had come from. They were sure, that flight connected two lovebirds. He flew the Cub like Lizzie did. Okay, he kept his wings on but landed short and sweet. John and Lizzie got back quite a bit before they did. Sure, Lizzie was faster, but she was sure Jake just thought it was the only way he could have Juliana to himself. Flying that slow bird. They all had a great week showing Jake about. He was quite impressed that Lizzie was the one who managed things for the lab, of course with Sarah's supervision. Jake was the one who brought up college and got everyone talking about where Lizzie might go.

"What do you want to do with your life?" he had asked her. No one had ever asked Lizzie that and she assumed she would stay here at the ranch. It was an awesome place to have grown up. After Bao and she had the attempted kidnapping in Sao Paulo, it was brought up again. By then Juliana and Jake were an item, planning a wedding, and the wedding would be the last thing Lizzie would do before going back to California to attend University.

People came from all over for the celebration. Brazilian weddings tend to be big events and with Jake's friends in Sao Paulo, and important associates spread out around the world, John and Sarah went all out. Juliana, for all practical purposes, had become a part of the family. John loved Juliana and Sarah wanted to give Juliana the wedding of her dreams. John couldn't have been happier to have the best of both worlds. As far as he was concerned this just gave him the family he had wished for. Two hundred people came for a three-day extravaganza. Lizzie had to wear a dress since she was the maid of honor. It was fun seeing some of her parent's old friends. There were a few kids her age, but they seemed more interested in sneaking champagne and smoking cigarettes, neither of which interested Lizzie. As soon as she could, she wished the happy couple best wishes forever, gave huge hugs to all, got a ride to the airport, and flew the Stearman home in the dress. Chuck happened to see Lizzie getting her preflight done and whistled. She could have killed him. Lizzie scowled and gave him the bird.

"Whoa, little missy," he said, "no harm meant, just never saw you in a dress before. And is that mascara I see? Good grief girl, makeup now? Nice shoes, new fashion statement?"

Lizzie checked the oil and threw the rag at him. "Stop it!" she shouted. She couldn't wait to get out of that dress and back in camo shorts. She'd already taken off those horrible 3-inch heels and had her high-top blue converse tennis shoes on and her Oakland A's baseball cap.

Those memories seemed so long ago.

Right now, she was heading back to Sao Paulo to find Juliana and the twins. Lizzie could imagine what Jake was feeling. Lizzie had felt that way too, once, a long time ago. Captain Pete announced they would be landing in a few minutes. Joy reminded her to put her seatbelt on. Lizzie knew she didn't need it; these two guys were the smoothest in the business. She was wrong—they had to do an immediate go around as a troop of monkeys had wandered out onto the runway and they would have to go into a holding pattern until the tarmac was cleared. It felt a lot like Tanzania, where zebras and warthogs had a habit of wandering out on the runway too. Things had been uneventful for years, but as they say, things come in threes, and change was coming. Fast.

Chapter 9

Saving Juliana

Joy opened the door to the Gulf 3 and the warm humid Sao Paulo air rolled in. Lizzie thanked Pete and Rick for a fine go-around, happy that they had saved one more monkey pod for Brazil. Lizzie could see Bao standing by the Orchid hanger. Always easy to spot; if he wanted to be spotted that is. He looked buff like he had been working out and put on some weight finally. His face angry, lips tight, dark eyes intent. Blue shirt, jeans, and his favorite Oakland A's green and yellow baseball cap on, dark strands of hair curling out. John and he were frequent fans anytime they got the chance. Lizzie got the hat; she never really got the game. For Bao, it was so American, baseball, and all that. Bao never let an opportunity go by to remind her how lucky she was to be an American. Even though he was Khmer, it was long ago, and he had worked hard to be a citizen of the U.S., tricky, but it did happen. Of course, there was no going back to Cambodia for him. For all practical purposes, he didn't really exist there. He was as close to a son as John had and his loyalty to the family, and obviously the Oakland A's was unquestionable. That hat, or a version of it, was usually on his head during family time. Lizzie loved seeing her dad and Bao with their hats on, especially turned backward. That meant the Oakland A's had won that day. On those days it was like anyone else winning a million bucks! Pure joy those two shared, all over a ball… The hat on forward meant they still had work to do, and that Chuck was standing by him and not by Jake, meant they didn't have Juliana and the twins back yet.

Everybody, half-heartedly, hugged, more concerned to get to the work on hand. Bao led them immediately inside Orchid's Flight Base Operations. The Orchid International FBO had turned into a "SWAT" base. The large office was lit up like a space station with five people at computers—big screens and databases were whirling. Lizzie had never seen anything like this outside of the *Hawaii 5-0* shows she watched occasionally in the States, late at night when she couldn't sleep. She loved Kono and the complexity of her role with "Five." Looking at the room, John had spared no expense, and from the look of things, Chuck was in charge here. Men in jungle fatigues with an assortment of Glock pistols, Walthers, and other 45s strapped to them, stood around the room watching Chuck. Waiting for their orders. Each guy had a table with an assortment of weapons they were checking. One had a Colt M4, another an MP5/10 submachine gun. Lots of night gear, GPNV6 night vision goggles. Wherever the twins were, it would be a war that would get them out, if it came down to that. Lizzie knew Orchid International, and Genesis had occasion to flex their muscles. She had seen a lot of these weapons over the years when accompanying her father into dangerous areas. She had seen too many in Africa, just around the medical camps and border crossings. She knew how to use a gun—Chuck made sure of that since they spent so much time flying over and being in the jungle. Her dad gave her a Smith & Wesson Shield when he gave her the Stearman. "In case you go down somewhere Honey, it's good to have some protection," he said. These were different men than she had seen before, but they were obviously men that Chuck knew and trusted. Still, she wished she had her own gun too.

Their team had narrowed down their enemy, quickly, once the leak was found. Someone knew when to get the girls. The leak was Anna, Juliana's new assistant.

Anna had a story herself. The police were never even called when Anna went missing. Her father had given her to Diego, who lied, and said he would marry her. That he loved her. Her father could not afford to care for her and his other children. He hoped Diego would. Within a month Diego had begun sharing her with his friends who would repeatedly rape her. Then he would beat her if she would not have sex with men for money. She hurt so much from the beatings and the rapes that eventually she agreed to the crack cocaine, which made the pain go away for a while. Quickly addicted she went along with the abuse. After her drug use escalated, Diego said she cost too much to keep, and he sold her to another pimp. He moved her to another town for a while but returned her to Sao Paulo after a year. By then she was 15. Addicted to cocaine and sickly, Victor, her new owner, sold her sometimes twenty times a day. Now, he too tired of her. It was common for pimps to trade girls or sell them. He sold her to a man who took her away, to get better, to work in his house he said. Not true, he took her to a village where she was supposed to work the fields by day and whore by night. When she was too tired, he beat her. Her ribs were broken—his men had gang-raped her and then kicked her a few times for good measure. She was a completely broken girl.

They thought she was dead and had dumped her off on the road. The next day she was found in an embankment along the road, bruised, beaten, eyes swollen shut, bloodied and naked. A priest who was driving to Sao Paulo stopped to relieve himself and saw her body lying in the embankment. After putting her in the car, he drove her directly to Sao Paulo, to Juliana's shelter, Lady of Hope. Juliana was there the day Anna came in. All knew her way-too-common story. Some were saved, but many went back out for fear of what might happen to their families if they didn't return. Some, because now they knew nothing else, or the withdrawals were too much to handle. Most died from disease, drugs, or suicide within seven years of being put into the sex trafficking trade. It was hard to stop such a lucrative business. The product was endless. When one wore out, you just found another to sell. Billions of dollars in the industry. The consumers, vast and insatiable.

Diego and Victor found out that Anna was in the shelter and was working for Juliana. They threatened her. She panicked. She gave them a time and location for Juliana, which is how they got her and the girls. When Diego had called, he wanted three million dollars, "One million' for each chickee," he said, "tonight at the docks or they would be shipped out," most likely to Germany where Brazilian girls get big money. Pier 48. 10 p.m. Bring the money and we will give you the woman and the girls. No one but Jake. They knew what he looked like—he was in the papers all the time.

"No police, no funny business, or we will kill them all. No, we will do worse, and you will never see them again," said the one with the gravelly voice, coughing into the phone, every sentence ending with a hack and a cough, a sound that Chuck used to identify them with his asset's knowledge.

Jake wanted to hear them, Chuck wanted proof they were still alive and asked for Jake to talk to them. The girls each spoke, crying and afraid, but said they were OK. Of course, Diego would not want to damage the merchandise. Juliana's voice did not waiver when Jake spoke to her. He could not know she was hurt from fighting back, her lips swollen, her nose broke, one eye shut, and clothes shredded. They would later learn she would do whatever to protect her girls, her bargaining distracting the men temporarily.

They had no plans on touching them. Virgins like these were extremely valuable. Victor and Diego wanted to make sure Jake understood he had to do whatever it took for the money to arrive untraceable and in larger denominations. Not so easy to trade. Stupid men. Chuck and his team would soon send them back to the hell-spawn from which they must have come. One way or another.

"Lizzie, I know you love them and would do anything to save them, but right now we need you to be quiet and listen. We need you here for when we bring them back. You don't know anything about combat and these men are the best at what they do. Please trust Chuck."

Lizzie finally got the idea of what Chuck really did in the world. These were his men and women. They were trained killers. Ex-Navy Seals, guns for hire, mercenaries. Lizzie always kind of knew there was another side to Chuck because he would disappear every so often. Returning with new scars and injuries, complaining he was getting too old for this and should just take up charters full-time. He never really said what he was too old for and Lizzie never asked. She didn't need to ask now, that's for sure. By five minutes after ten, Chuck and his mercenaries had eliminated Victor, Diego, and their henchmen. Police would find the bodies the next day, blame it on gang violence or a drug deal gone wrong. Looked like the war zone they planned. Take no prisoners. Leave a message. Think twice before you kidnap anyone in our clan.

Jake and Bao took Juliana and the girls to a private hospital where they met Lizzie. Bao called ahead and had Lizzie waiting there for them. There would be no police report, John and Jake would see to that. Juliana looked bad, and yes, she needed Lizzie's medical attention as well as her love. In the short time, they had Juliana, they had punched her, played tick-tac toe on her belly with a sharp knife, and repeatedly raped her, not particularly in that order. She would do anything for them not to hurt the girls. Jake and Juliana's private physician checked them all out thoroughly. The girls were physically intact, too valuable to Victor and Diego, unlike poor Juliana. Lizzie stayed with the girls for their examinations. They had been privy to their mother's screams and the nasty insults of Diego and Victor towards her. They knew their mother had done all she could to save them, but they would never know what Lizzie knew. Juliana was just a toy to them and a way to push Jake for more money. They never intended for her to live. The pictures they had painted with their words of what they did to Juliana sealed the fate of every man in that gang. Muerto. Death. They had no idea who they had messed with, they had no idea what they had awoken. Something in Lizzie, as well, awoke that day. Something dark and dangerous that had been simmering for a while. Tired of the abuse she had seen, too many times, too many places, over the years.

They all tried to rest at Jake and Juliana's home in the hills of Sao Paulo for a few days and then flew out on the Gulf 3 with Rick, Pete, and Joy as their crew to Oakland, California. Juliana didn't want anyone to ever know what had happened. Just Lizzie and Jake would know. Juliana was incredibly strong. She would take her anger and hatred and attack the traffickers the only way she knew, by healing others worse off than her, helping them at the Lady of Hope. She would never be able to have any more children from the damage they did to her, but spiritually she would heal. Her kidnappers were dead. Some scars and occasionally nightmares her only memory. Her girls were safe. Her family intact. In Juliana's eyes, God had saved them. In Lizzie's eyes, Juliana lost her future children, her home in Sao Paulo, the Lady of Hope. Chuck and his men had taken care of the threat for now.

Now all were going off to Oakland to the Lakehouse, where John's small family had run from long ago. But this time they ran to it for Juliana and the girls. This time Sarah would be waiting for them and she would have plenty to do with her new full house. The news reported that at midnight, a night watchman had found dozens of dead bodies of known sex traffickers and their paid thugs, at Pier 48. No one really cared about Victor or Diego. Many celebrated their demise. Chuck and the men just disappeared like the ghosts of the night that they were, and neither Orchid International nor Genesis would ever be associated with any of it.

They flew through the night and Lizzie awoke with the City by the Bay outside her window. It had been a while since she called Oakland her home. With all of them together again, maybe now it might just feel like a real home again at the lake. She wished on that big golden gate bridge, sneaking thru the fog, that it would be so. Her mother used to do that, she recalled.

"We could all use a lot of normal, whatever that was," thought Lizzie.

Chapter 10

Returning Home

They arrived early, a foggy sunrise over San Francisco, landing at Oakland International Airport. Joy had the coffee Lizzie had given her on the flight from Arusha, brewing for them; a deep, strong, sweet acacia berry-like scented coffee with notes of cedar. Smelled fantastic! Reminding Lizzie that just a few days ago she was in Arusha with her friendly albino folks. She would have to check in with Kathryn and let her know they had rescued the twins and Juliana. That everyone was safe. Including Lizzie. Kathryn had become such a good friend. Lizzie knew someday she would go back there, but until then she would just have to enjoy the coffee. Amazing, once again, how Joy knew just what to give her to flip a switch. The twins had blueberry muffins with tons of butter and hot cocoa, covered with fresh cream. Juliana needed a good cup of coffee too—more than anything she wanted to be awake for the arrival. Lizzie tried to give her an Ambien, but Juliana wouldn't even agree to take a new non-narcotic sleeping pill, even though the company her husband was CEO of now, marketed them. Juliana would have nightmares every time she would try to sleep, and Lizzie would wake up to hear Juliana moaning. Jake had hardly left her side since they got her back from the devil's keep. He accepted a steamy cup of coffee from Joy too. They just nibbled on a little fruit and cheese. Lizzie warned them her mom would have a huge brunch for them at the house. It would be good to all sit together in the big dining room, the fires burning on each end of the room, warming them up after their foggy arrival. They all knew each other, but now they would live under the same roof for a time. A new family gathering. Hopefully, a healing time for all.

Jake's family had never been to the Lakehouse but had heard stories about how lovely the lake and gardens were. All were looking forward to being somewhere else for a while. Sao Paulo was a haunted place for them right now, full of masked men and black Escalades with dark windows. The Lakehouse had been full of ghosts for the Harmen's when they left after Lilly's death. They knew the feeling. Bao and John thought it best that they all be out of Brazil for a few months, at the very least. They really didn't know if there would be any repercussions from Diego and Victor's people if indeed they had any people left. Scuttle on the street was that Diego had messed with the wrong people and a kidnapping attempt on a rich influential family had gone the wrong direction for them. Very few kidnappings ended well for the victims. They usually lost the money or the abductee, or both. This might be food for thought for the next attempt on a Sao Paulo family. Full-time guards were put outside Our Lady of Hope. Chuck had just the guys, recently retired but still wanting to protect something. Of course, when Juliana returned someday, she would always have security. Jake and Chuck made sure of that. Juliana would not give up her work. Now she was even more adamant than before she would fight this battle. In her eyes, it just became more personal than before.

After going through the customs holding area, better known as the "penalty box," they were checked by Homeland Security with all their passports and documents in order. The captain, crew, and passengers' names and dates checked, thoroughly sniffed for bombs and who knows what, they were then allowed to taxi over to the Orchid hanger where their rides home awaited them. Travel certainly wasn't as easy as it once was…still it sure beats commercial, which Lizzie still did when traveling abroad. She had forgotten about all these luxuries.

On arrival, with the doors of the hanger wide open, Sarah was standing there waiting for them. For so long, Sarah had mourned Lilly, and Oakland was the reminder of that time for her still sometimes. Lizzie guessed that in swiftly having to prepare for Julianna and the girls, preparing to fill the house and gardens with children again, Lakeside would come alive again. God only knows they needed Sarah right now.

72

Maybe Sarah needed them too. She had said the house needed some filling up. She was needed to ready things for them and was the only one who could organize the house as it should be for the new family. Sarah had driven herself to the airport in her old green Range Rover and her new assistant, Jenny, was driving one of Orchid International's pearl-colored Cadillac Escalades with the pink flowers on it, mostly used for corporate stuff, but sometimes for hauling company around.

Lizzie had been at the Lakehouse now and then, mostly just passing through on her way to the next job. She knew Sarah was adding on but had no idea the scale of additions she had accomplished in the past two years! Sarah had been extremely busy it seemed! The boathouse was gone and in its place was a huge greenhouse and along it a newly planted arboretum with trees even Lizzie hadn't seen before. She had eliminated the place where Lilly had died and built a twenty-five-meter-high greenhouse, with a canopy of colored glass and sculpted metal. Lizzie had never seen anything like it, outside of France.

Bao smiled, "If she couldn't be in Brazil anymore, we brought it to her. Yes, Lizzie, all her Brazilian favorites are in there, some Cambodian species too, Cookie says. It was quite a feat getting them into the country, but you know your dad, he'd do anything for her."

Lizzie wondered, perhaps that's why customs was sniffing them out so closely? It had been a long time since Lizzie wanted to stay at the Lakehouse. She had lived in tents and adobe huts for the last couple of years. She was ready for some comforts of home. And what a homecoming it was turning out to be! Bao obviously knew about this all along and had never said anything. John had built a guest house down by the lake that Lizzie just heard of now from Bao. Lizzie couldn't believe they had kept this a secret! She realized now it had been years since she had been home, but still, from the size of the plants, you would think she had been gone a hundred years. Sarah's seriously magic green thumb was still doing its wonders.

And not just the greenhouse. As they drove past it and up the road, Lizzie could see that Sarah had added a whole new wing to the house! The main house was pretty much the same outside and the inside had lots of updates and fresh country colors. Come to think of it, the whole thing looked French country. Lizzie had grown up in a Tudor mansion until she was twelve, lived on a Brazilian farm in the jungle, and now they had a French country house smack in the middle of the Bay Area. A wonderful surprise. It did explain Sarah's attitude. It was kind of a new place but the same wonderful old faces. Cookie was standing at the front door. She had been old when Lizzie was born so she couldn't imagine how old she was now. There was a little Spanish woman and handsome young man standing next to her. Abilo was his name, and she was Antonia. They were from Sao Paulo! They were Sarah's new helpers along with Cookie's, who, for all practical purposes, needed looking after herself these days. The new family would need them all.

Juliana had been in some beautiful homes in Sao Paulo. She had lived in one of the oldest and nicest neighborhoods there, but it was nothing like this. The twins soon found the ballroom and were doing pirouettes! Sarah was beaming. In the old days, she would have had someone else show you to your rooms, but now she was so excited, she did it herself. She wanted to show them, Lizzie thought, really wanted them all to feel welcome in their new home. And so, leading them all to their suites was her way of starting. In her own way, she had cleansed the ghosts. It was not the same place Lizzie had grown up in and left a part of her heart and soul years ago. And that was fine by her. All was fresh and new. So maybe life could be too.

Antonia, Cookie, and Abilo all stayed in the old part of the house where Sarah, John, Lilly, and Lizzie had been. Sarah had let them decorate their rooms themselves. Sarah referred to this wing as the Buddhist/Catholic quarters. They each had made a shrine to their Gods. They could see the lake from this side of the house and part of the greenhouse. Cookie had set up a kind of shrine at the end of their hallway with a smiling Buddha on it and candles burning. The Brazilians had little Mary of Nazareth and Jesus statues accompanying them.

At the top stair, you turned left to go towards "Cookie's East" wing, to the right was the entry to the new west wing. First, there was a small sitting area with four yellow checkered, severely overstuffed chairs, surrounding a puzzle table, a small library, and computer desk with two computers already waiting nearby. There was a TV hidden behind a cabinet, with an assortment of games, movies, and such for the girls. The west wing was a trio of bedroom suites, each with its own bathroom. One had a small office/sitting room. Juliana and Jake would have this room. The girls across from them, leaving the other bedroom for someone else. Sarah and John had a huge master suite on the main floor now. It looked out to a new garden and a sparkling blue pool with a waterfall on one end that fondly reminded Lizzie of a place on the river, at the ranch they used to swim in as a family. Sarah's bathroom was a beautiful small greenhouse of its own, with a gorgeous claw foot tub, surrounded by small palm trees and zillions of tiny white and red lacy orchids. Lizzie forgot what they were called; they reminded her of something, but she couldn't recall just then. She would be sure to ask her mom. In the meantime, Lizzie was dying to see the new guest house cabin. Her and Bao's home when they were here. Home? What was that anymore to her? The Lakehouse? A tent? And adobe huts? Home was where the heart was—and everyone she loved was here. Sarah found her and saw her looking towards the cabin.

"It has two suites, a living room, and a kitchen. We thought you and Bao would like your own place when you were here. He has enjoyed it."

Lizzie stared at Bao. How could he have kept this a secret?

"Your bug's parked down there."

"You kept my Volkswagen?" Lizzie had forgotten about it. She drove that back in San Francisco when she was in school. Lizzie hadn't really driven much since. But she did like the bug. Easy to park in the city. Anywhere.

Sarah had to show the house off first and then Lizzie could go to the cabin and freshen up before they met for brunch. As they entered the new rooms, everyone complemented Sarah on her design work. Lizzie couldn't help but notice the family's new rooms all faced the pool, not the lake. She was okay with that. Still, she was curious to see what was in the greenhouse and to check out the new cabin. She headed out for a look-see while everyone got settled. They would all meet again later for their first "new family" brunch. Lizzie went out to explore the new additions. Bao had business he needed to attend to, excused himself, and went into John's office, quietly closing the door behind him.

After Sarah's amazing tour, she released all to their prospective rooms, and then Lizzie waved "later gator" and headed towards the cabin. The cabin was truly a surprise! It looked like the pictures she had seen of the cabin in Oregon, very rustic, but obviously modernized. A great room in the middle of the two suites, with a huge rock fireplace, a crackling fire already warming the room, a worn leather couch, and big burgundy leather reading chairs. She recognized the couch and chairs from the library in the house. Her mom knew she always loved them. One wall was covered floor to ceiling with books already, but still room for new ones. A window seat with a peek of the lake through the old forest. The porch wrapped around with matching white rockers in front and back. A small kitchen with just the basics, Black Butte Porter from Oregon, an espresso maker with Arusha coffee, a fridge, and a small Wolf range. The pots hung over the island. The fridge contained lox, cream cheese, butter, and fruit. There was a fresh loaf of French bread from La Boulangerie on the counter. Sarah knew Lizzie would love that. She peeked in one of the bedrooms; this one was obviously Bao's. A huge desk, with a cabinet behind it. The only real luxury in there was the rich silk bedding from Thailand that he loved and a huge walk-in steam shower. He had a few things in the closet. Three Armani suits, Italian shoes, A's caps, blue sweatshirt, and his boat shoes. The second bedroom was much larger and had barn doors that opened so you could leave them open and see the fireplace. Her private bath had a tub with an old-style rain showerhead and curtain by a window looking out to a grove of eucalyptus. The closet organizer had a few of her things she had left years ago, already hung or folded in it. The tall double bed covered with the softest Turkish- cotton bedding and a plush-down comforter. No mosquito nets! A couple of photos of her and the Stearman. One of her waving from the cockpit, another of her and Chuck the day she first flew it, sat on a shelf. Some photos of Africa she had sent home, from places she told them were her favorites. There were lots of favorites.

This was to be Lizzie's place when she came home. Lizzie would have her privacy and so would Bao. It would be nice to have a place for themselves, she thought. Bao was rarely here, he traveled constantly, so it's not like they would be there together all that often. They would sit on the porch, catch up on life before Juliana's kidnapping, and what was next. She knew he would be careful with his questions but also much more direct than her parents. It would be interesting to look at the lake from this new perspective. A lot had happened in the last 12 years. They had killed enough demons by now, right? It had been a long time since they had really been alone, just the two of them. It would be good to see where their lives had taken them these past few years. Bao was the one person she could talk to about anything. Right?

Chapter 11

Emergency Rooms and Tattoos

Although the circumstances that brought them all back to Oakland and the Lakehouse had been terrifying, a new chapter in all their lives seemed to be about to start. After a few weeks, Juliana and Jake decided it was best that the girls stay and go to Bentley, a private school started in 1920, that Sarah, and then Lizzie and Lilly had attended. They could stay at the Lakehouse if they wished. Lizzie hadn't lived in the States much since leaving USF and thought she'd give it a go and stick around awhile too. She applied for a position in the E.R. at Highland Hospital in Oakland, a primary trauma center and county hospital. It had been affiliated with UCSF and she had spent some time there in residency. After working with minimum staff and resources in South America and Africa it seemed like the Hilton of hospitals. Anyone who lived in the Bay Area knew it wasn't. Most patients lacked insurance and there were plenty of illegals with low to no income that walked through the doors. They call these kinds of hospitals "safety nets." No one is turned away. Lizzie saw some ugly stuff there and some amazing heroics amongst the staff, the same as on her missions. Tough world out there. Tough docs and nurses. Most with hearts of gold going in, hardened going out. The turnover rate was huge. It was easy for Lizzie to get hired with few questions. No one would have thought someone with her background would be working there. It gave her the anonymity she always craved.

Lizzie felt right at home, the long haulers had worked missions too, they knew how to use what they had, sometimes bend the rules to get what they needed and when to look away. They knew they could save some, but mostly, lots of band-aids were applied. Much of the diseases here were social. Poverty breeds desperation, abandonment, and hopelessness. There were lots of drug overdoses, gang violence, and abuses of all kinds. Lizzie would work long hours and return to the same story the next day, different faces, same place. She struggled with how in a country that had so much, they still had so many social ills. The homeless situation was out of control. Lizzie stayed too long at Highland. She usually moved around from mission to mission every sixty to ninety days. Lizzie stayed a year at Highland, enough time to know she wasn't going to change anything there. At least not this way.

Over the year, Lizzie had made a few friends. Sarah and Juliana tried to set her set up on dates, which Lizzie would somehow manage to squeeze out of at the last minute. They gave up after they found out Lizzie had gone out with some folks from work to watch a soccer game at a local pub after work. Guess that was enough for them to deem her not entirely antisocial. Her circle had always been family, flying, the farm, school, and missions. Lizzie would always say she had no time for a relationship. She moved too often to develop anything. She brushed men off so quickly, they left her alone. The truth was Lizzie could not imagine being with anyone. She told herself she had enough to do, that what someone might ask of her she couldn't do. Bao never had dated that she knew of and no one ever said anything about that. Juliana would tease her about the way she dressed, calling her style early Eddie Bauer Fishing or Earhart Flying Club. The last time she had a dress on was at Juliana and Jake's wedding and she had hated the way Chuck had teased her as she jumped up into the Stearman to fly back to the ranch, the propeller wind blowing her dress up showing off her standard "not sexy" cotton underpants. In her mind, she still saw Lilly's little yellow dress floating up around her. Lizzies' scrubs and crocs at the hospital were what she felt normal in. Shorts, khakis, her hair pulled under baseball caps. Bomber jacket. Hoodies. Flip flops.

Her normal these days she referred to as "The Daily Crisis," the recurring soap opera at the hospital. One morning at the end of her shift, a Spanish couple and a little girl hurried into the E.R. The woman looked like so many she had seen at the Lady of Hope. She was past trafficking age but had the same haunted, empty look in her eyes. The man stayed right by her, holding her arm a little too tightly, the little girl's shoulder held with his other hand. Her nose was bleeding, one eye closed shut; you could see she had tried to wipe her face. The tears running down her face were bloody still. Her arm dangling at an unnatural angle, and Lizzie could see right away it was broken. None of them seemed to speak English. In Spanish, he said they were her guardians, that the parents were still in Mexico. Lizzie's Spanish came in very handy here in the E.R. No doubt the information the staff had taken was fake. Lizzie's load was light that morning and something was whispering in her mind to give this one more attention. Eric, the chief E.R. doc, pretty much let the female nurses or nurse practitioners, like Lizzie, deal with these kinds of patients. The Mexicans didn't like men touching their girls, anyway, and would allow only nurses to treat them. Lizzie lied and told them that only the staff could be there to fix her arm and to wait in the waiting room. The couple said the girl had fallen down some stairs at their apartment. When she examined the girl, she said she hurt all over. Lizzie asked her where she hurt the most and she pointed to her bottom. The tears welled up and she knew, even before looking, what she would find. Although she looked like an 8-year-old, she said she was 11, she thought but wasn't sure if her birthday had passed. The girl was so malnourished. Her arm was fractured. She had a slight concussion. When Lizzie went to do a vaginal exam, the first thing she noted was the tattoo on the girl's inner thigh. She had seen this before. A small bull, obviously a mark of ownership to some gang. The last girl she saw with this bull had been gang-raped, somehow had escaped, and found her way here. After testing for STDs and being given Zithromax for gonorrhea, she had disappeared. They hadn't seen her again, but Lizzie was the one there that day. She had seen these kinds of tattoos in Brazil, when there were two alike, it presented a pattern. Somebody had a stable of little bulls.

Lizzie gently asked the standard, nonthreatening, questions as she examined the child. Her fluid Spanish made these situations so much better, but still, it was sensitive grounds. You wanted to gather as much information as possible in case DHS or the police showed up.

"Your name is Maria?"

"Yes, Senora," she shyly responded.

"Have you had a period yet?"

"Yes," she said quietly, "two times."

"When was the last one?"

"Maybe three months ago," she said, "And then I started bleeding a lot the last few days."

"Lots of cramping?"

"Yes," she says.

"More than before?"

" Yes," she looked down.

"Does it hurt here?" Lizzie presses gently on her abdomen.

"It did, but it went away." She wouldn't look Lizzie in the eye. The vaginal and rectal exam showed bruising plus evidence of blunt force trauma. Lizzie collected swabs and trace evidence for a sexual assault kit as best she could. Lizzie was sure they forced an abortion on her with something. There are signs of forced rape in the last 24 hours. She had seen this too many times in Africa. The girl was lucky, there was no permanent damage she could see, physically anyway. When Lizzie was in Africa, in the Congo, she had seen young child brides who had given birth too young or raped repeatedly, with a condition called a vaginal fistula, which causes urinary problems and fecal incontinence. These girls are then abandoned to live in shame and embarrassment if not treated. Lizzie knew the cost to repair such damage is prohibitive in many third-world countries. Here in the U.S., it can be treated surgically, often by laparoscopy, at a cost of around $7,000 to $8,000. It is too expensive in the Congo—militia men just find another young wife. They toss the damaged ones aside, like so much garbage. No one will marry them after they are damaged. They are thus not useful to the men. It's a horrible fate and insane that it still goes on, but it's changing as more people became aware of it.

Lizzie left the girl with an aide and went out to talk to the couple. The woman asked, "if the girl is pregnant or has the disease?" she seems to have no other concern for the girl. Nada.

"No," Lizzie tells her, "but it is very probable she has been pregnant, and someone aborted her from what she has told me. She will need to stay and be treated for a few hours. I'll need to talk to her for a few minutes and I'll be right back."

Lizzie asked the girl who has had sex with her. She says only the man. Lizzie tells her she is too young, and they are breaking the law, that the hospital has people that can help her. "We can get you help." Lizzie thinks human trafficking. She wonders about The Lady of Hope.

The girl shakes her head. No. But she is a minor and she has no choice.

When Lizzie goes back out to tell the couple. They are gone. Fine with her.

Two hours pass. The front desk said the woman told them she would be back shortly, but they never returned. Should she call the number they left? Yes, but of course it was a disconnected number. For once Lizzie may get to keep one and find out what this little bull tattoo means. Maria says she got it last year, right after the first time they first started using her. The woman said she had to have the tattoo so everyone would know who she belonged to. That she must let the man have her if she wanted to eat. If she fought, they would put her out in the streets where it would be much worse for her. She had not seen her mother for a long time. She overheard them say she was 'on the streets in Mexico.' It will be a while before Lizzie hears about Maria again. She is a lucky one—she is still young and child services take her that night. She lets Juliana know. Immigration is sure to step in before long. Juliana has connections.

Before Lizzie is on shift again, she stops to watch a game with some residents from UCSF at a nearby pub. She rarely drinks alcohol, but she does enjoy a good pizza and the occasional black butte porter. It's always fun to hear the excitement the residents still have in the early years of comradery. She asks if any of them have seen this little bull tattoo? She shows them a picture she sketched and then copied to her phone. "Yes," one woman says, "I have seen this at Kaiser ER in San Jose and the East Palo Alto planned parenthood clinic." Another resident says he has seen this tattoo at Highland too. It's not like they have a ton of time to gossip at the hospital, nor do they read each other's charts all the time. Lizzie tells them about Maria and the girl with the little bull tattoo. There is absolutely a pattern here.

Lizzie got a call two days later from one of the residents, that a Hispanic teenage girl was at the hospital and they didn't expect her to make it. She had a little bull on her inner thigh. Another gang rape or something else? The police brought her in after a dock worker found her on his way to the boats. She said she had tried to escape because they were about to take her north. Several had taken their turns with her, before discarding her by the wetlands near the docks. They thought she would sink in the muck. They assumed she was dead. She pretended to be and crawled out as they sped away. She could barely talk, and maybe not for long. Lizzie understood what the resident was saying. The police had dropped her off, did some quick paperwork, and left for another emergency, a double homicide just a few miles away. A normal night in Oakland. The hospital would follow up with the proper authorities after dealing with the girl's injuries if they could figure out who she was. She had no identification. Nobody had claimed her. There were no missing persons reported about her that matched.

Lizzie grabbed her keys and rushed to work. She had plenty of time before her shift to check into this. She was really getting tired of these throw-away girls. Little bull tattoos or not.

Chapter 12

First Time Feels So Good

It was already getting dark when Lizzie's shift started. She had snatched a small vial of devil's breath powder from Sarah's lab. They had tested it on some mice, not long ago, just to see for themselves if it really did what they heard it would. The mice turned into little zombies and then dropped dead in just seconds. There was enough there to surely knock a human out. Lizzie had an idea, and hopefully an opportunity.

As Lizzie was walking through the far parking lot, she saw the couple who had brought in little Maria the week before, arguing by an old, dented, blue Ford work van.

The man was yelling at the mocha-skinned woman, who once may have been lovely, but now was just short, worn, and angry looking. "Puta get in there and get her. One of the guys I left her with last night said he saw them bring her in. He went back to get her, saw the ambulance take her, and followed them to the hospital. She needs to be dead or out of there immediately before she says something." He had no idea how badly they had hurt her this time or that they had left her to die. The woman walked back into the hospital, scared of going inside but terrified of staying out with him. The man swore some more, with words even Lizzie was sure she had rarely heard in Spanish or English. Neither of them noticed Lizzie, as they were too busy yelling at each other. Before he got back in the van, the man pulled his hair back into a ponytail. Lizzie saw the little bull tattoo on his neck. Leader of the gang? It was the same tattoo that was on the girls. The man got in the passenger side of the van, rolled down the window, swore some more to himself, and reclined. Lizzie had seen how he treated Maria and the fear both women had in their eyes towards him. Damn pimp. Traffickers. Creep. Stupid enough to show up here again.

Lizzie turned and followed the woman back into the hospital, nodding to a few staff members as she went along. She noted what room the woman had gone into, picked up the file in the door, and scanned it quickly. Noted a "small bull tattoo" on the girls' inner right thigh. Bingo. Gotcha.

The next room had just been vacated with a small, but very sharp scalpel left on the tray. Lizzie put it into her pocket. These go missing more often than hospitals would like you to know, it was sad to say. Opportunity was knocking hard, pounding in Lizzie's heart and brain. The woman was sitting talking to the nurse in the sitting room. The nurse was telling her it would be a little while before the patient could go, maybe overnight.

Staff was stalling until they could get DHS to come over. The little bull tattoo had triggered a lot of questions. Lizzie would not have much time.

Without a second thought, she grabbed a large green scrub pulling it quickly over her own flowered one, then pocketed a couple of surgical gloves, quickly slipped on a cap, booties, and a mask. No one would notice her amongst the crowd of like outfits. She hurried outside into the dark, the people changing shifts would think she was just another exhausted resident in a hurry to get out of there. She had pictured this in her mind before, but never had the guts to do it. This night would be different. Opportunity only knocks once.

Lucky for Lizzie, no other cars were parked by the van, except a few medical supply trucks that would be going out in the morning, and a dumpster. There was a cool fog drifting in from the bay settling towards the parking lot. When she got to the van the man looked like he was sleeping, his head on the door, the window open, snoring. Lizzie reached in her pocket, slid off the cap of the vile, and tossed the deadly powder in his face. Startled, he inhaled the powder quickly and immediately panicked, breathing it in heavily. His throat constricted quickly, and he found himself unable to move or speak. Pleased at his reaction, Lizzie reached over and with a quick flick of her wrist slit his throat with the scalpel, cutting through his carotid artery and the jugular vein. Hot red blood splashed. She pushed him over between the seats. Death came so quickly. He never really knew what had happened to him, his last vision, a face with gold speckled amber eyes that looked vaguely familiar. His eyes wide open in disbelief with a sense he knew this woman. Angel of death? No, someone he'd seen before, for sure. The last face he would ever see.

Blood on Lizzie! She took the green scrub off quickly, ripped off the mask, wrapped it, the surgical gloves, booties, vial, and scalpel all in a small brown plastic Safeway bag she had stashed in her pocket. She walked over to the dumpster tossing the bag over the edge, like yesterday's left-over lunch, smiling as she saw the garbage truck company coming around the corner to pick up the dumpster. She really was a lucky lady tonight.

Going back into the hospital, Lizzie checked in for the night shift. Washed her hands and face, checked her scrubs for any splatter. Not like that would be something anyone would take note of, but still… The whole process of getting rid of Mr. Little Bull took twenty minutes, start to finish. She passed by the young girl's room, and the woman wasn't there. She probably overheard the staff talking about bringing in DHS and skedaddled. Most likely an illegal herself, she surely didn't want to get tied up in questioning. Lizzie would check in on the girl and see if Our Lady of Hope could help.

The woman had hung out in the waiting room for a while, the desk had said. Most likely not wanting to go out to the van to explain what was happening inside to the crazy man. Eventually, she left, just missing Lizzie on her way out. The woman gets in the van, finds her dead partner in a pool of blood. She has seen enough death, though his is a gift in disguise. He had brought them only trouble. She will be better off without him. She doesn't know who killed him, but the possibilities were endless. It is very dark out now, no moon, fog rolling in. She drives the van over to the bay. She parks under the bridge briefly, looking for a spot to dump the van. They had dumped a girl here before. Finding the right place, she grabs the backpack with their money, pilfers his wallet, then she turns the lights off, steps out, takes it out of park, and watches it roll into the bay and sink. She will have to find another van for the girls to sleep in. With this change of events, they will need to leave soon. She walks back to the avenues to gather the other girls.

The money she took out of Mr. Little Bull's wallet plus the cash and the dope in his backpack should get a car, several tanks of gas, food, and a motel away from here. She needed a shower and some clean clothes after dealing with him. She had blood on her hands. There would be more if she didn't get them out of here and soon. Another gang, the police, immigration, or DHS, any way you look at it, it was time to move on. Maybe the little bull tattoo can be modified to a little donkey she wondered?

Lizzie had known she had taken a huge risk today. After her shift, she worked in her mom's greenhouse, stopping in the lab to check that there was still some devil's breath left. She hadn't taken it all. She just needed to see it. If her mom noticed she would say she must have used more than she thought in her experiment. It really wasn't that interesting to her mom, so she most likely wouldn't ask. It sure was interesting to Lizzie now though. She falls asleep while reading some old journals about especially effective poisonous plants that her dad and mom had observed being used by the locals back in Columbia. The *borrachero* shrub from Columbia has a flower whose seeds, when ground, turn into "Devil's Breath," a powder that can be blown into someone's face, or better, put on a card, so when it touches the skin, it is absorbed quickly enough to turn the victim into a walking zombie. Thus, the term "zombie drug" is commonly used. This kind of thing could come in handy. Yes, indeed it had, thought Lizzie. Scalpels are messy. Lizzie hated guns. She was too little to overpower anyone for long. Then she remembered a moment in time a long time ago. Gregor's face sinking by the dock. Dark water. A zombie drug and some deep water would do the trick, she mused. One part sounded good. She knew a little about drowning a person—she had after all witnessed one once. And seen enough casualties of drownings.

In the E.R. they had dealt with drowning victims. She had heard enough about it that she knew cold water kept them down the longest.

If she didn't want to get caught— which of course, what decent avenger would— it would have to be really cold water. Lots to think about as she goes off to sleep. Like, could she really become a vigilante? Because that's what they call people who kill bad guys outside the law. Lizzie had a list she could easily compile from any E.R. shift she had worked in the last few years. The newspapers and the Web were full of them, as well.

She falls asleep and dreams. Rivers run deep and cold. Bodies sink beneath the ripples. She feels excited and satisfied. She is in her Stearman looking down at bodies sinking into the depths of the dark ocean now. Lizzie is sitting behind her in the back seat, and they laugh just like they used to. She feels a calling. It's time to leave Highland Hospital and the Lakehouse. She'll find a place with a river. A deep, dark, cold river. She knows what she must do now. She needs to get things in order and start traveling again. But this time to cities and towns here in the U.S. where she can do some real good for a change.

Chapter 13

Goodbyes

Lizzie's phone was ringing Bao's secret tone, just for her, Elton John's *Tiny Dancer*. Hopefully, Bao is calling to tell her he was coming home. They shared the cabin when he was there, but they still called to say they were coming. It was always fun when they got together. Now that he handled so much of John's private businesses he didn't travel quite as much. They did a lot from the main house office. Jake had taken on John's role and they had moved key people up in Brazil. It had been like having this big family they never knew; the girls coming home from school, John, Sarah, and all of them having meals together, often. It had been a year now at Highland, and that's a long time for a contract nurse. Lizzie usually only stayed in places three to six months. Being with the family, though, made it hard to leave. But now it was necessary. She wasn't taking any chances with anyone recognizing her again.

The "little bull" incident had awakened Lizzie. For some reason, no one at Highland had seen any more little bull tattoos that week. In some ways, Lizzie felt guilty since the girls had come there for treatment. With Lizzie killing the pimp in the parking lot, maybe that woman had told someone what happened. Not likely. All the same, the gang would have moved on. For sure she wasn't coming back to Oakland. Both she and Lizzie knew what had happened. The woman just didn't know why or who. Lizzie knew they were still treating trafficker's girls. But no little bulls there. Lizzie would move on to another town too. She regretted telling the family. Yet she also knew they would not be surprised. She was a known gypsy after all.

"I'm on my way home, don't leave," said Bao. Lizzie could hear from the tone of his voice something was wrong. With them, with her, it could be anything. The incident in Sao Paulo? Killing Gregor? Not likely. The thing about killing bad guys is no one really cares. Someone would thank you if they could. Lizzie didn't need a thank you. She was more than happy to oblige. Bao can't know anything about Lizzie's recent episode, and she hoped he never would. She was careful. It had been a week. No connection to her could be found.

"Ok, I'm listening, Bao, what's wrong?" Lizzie asked.

"I will be there in 10 minutes, don't leave. Don't talk to anyone until I get there."

Good grief, what could it be? She knew instantly when she saw him. Lizzie could see Bao had been crying, he looked ten years older. The last time she had seen him cry was when Lilly died. He wasn't angry, just horribly distraught.

"It's Dad, isn't it?" Lizzie says.

"Lizzie, it's your mom, dad, Pete, and the crew. They flew down to San Diego for lunch at the Hotel Del Coronado today."

"Yes, it's their anniversary," Lizzie says. Her dad had told her a week ago that he was surprising her mom. They had enjoyed lots of time there over the years, especially at the San Diego Zoo.

"The plane didn't make it in Lizzie. It went into the ocean off the coast of San Diego on approach. They called in engine trouble. It was a little cloudy but nothing they couldn't handle. We don't think it's sabotage, but with the issue in Brazil, it's not impossible. The coast guard was in the area, saw it go down, looks like they tried to do a sea landing, but it was rough out there. The plane sunk before the guard could get there. No one has seen any survivors. They are all gone, Lizzie. Pete was flying with a new guy. They were in the Citation. It had just been gone over and everything checked out. I'm so sorry." Bao sat down and put his head in his hands. They were his family too. The only ones he ever knew. Lizzie would have to tell the girls. Juliana and Jake were on their way but couldn't be there until tomorrow. Maybe by then they might find the black box and see what had happened. Oh, God! Lizzie didn't know what to do. So, she did what she always did—what needed to be done, with Bao at her side.

Lizzie gathered the staff. She and Bao told them together. They were all visibly shaken. Cookie collapsed in a chair, wailing, then whispering prayers to herself. She had never got in a plane since they came to the States and had always sworn that she never would. They asked them to be prepared to stay longer hours for a few weeks, as they would have a full house and lots of details to attend to. Sarah and John had known a lot of people from all walks of life. This would be a challenge, but one that together, they could all help with. There would have to be services here and in Sao Paulo for all to say goodbye to two people that were cherished and respected by so many. "How will I say my goodbyes?" Lizzie thought to herself, "I am all that is left."

She called the school and told them she would be coming to get the girls early and to please say nothing to them about anything, that they had a family emergency. She wasn't sure how long the news would hold off reporting who had crashed, and being they were a wealthy well-known family, it was going to get picked up. Lizzie had a staff member drive her in the Range Rover to pick up the girls herself. It would be on the news as soon it was announced whose plane had gone down, as Orchid was a very visible and well-liked international company. Okay, sometimes. Like all large corporations, sometimes they pissed people off.

Lizzie had kept her anonymity over the years. It might be hard to keep out of the press right now though. Lizzie just became one of the richest women in the United States and the press loved that stuff. Bao knew how she felt and assured her that he and Jason Hamlin, the family attorney, would be the front men. She hated having her photo taken, as had her parents. Now more than ever, her privacy was tantamount. Mandatory, thought Lizzie. No photographers. No press. She would not leave the estate. The episode at Highland should never be tracked to her, but she also didn't need her face connected in any way to that place.

All the details of the service were handled by Lizzie and Bao. A beautiful memorial to Sarah and John was done in the garden, with a lunch following in the ballroom. Each table had a pink orchid set upon it. Her mom would have loved it, surrounded by all her trees, fauna, and flowers. The Orchid International group was tight, a lot like the family. Less than a hundred friends and associates were picked for the farewell to a respected and beloved pair of individuals. The Oakland airport had more private jets land in the last twenty-four hours than they knew where to park them. Some were sent to San Francisco, where limos would meet them, bringing them to the Lakehouse. Parking had to be set up outside the gates, as chauffeurs waited for their employers to return from the services. Private police were hired to keep curious passerby or press moving along.

San Francisco's archbishop stood in front of a spectacular replica of a small waterfall John had proposed to Sarah at, in Brazil, so many years ago, surrounded by ancient redwoods, ferns, and deep green moss—the small creek bubbling behind the trees towards the lake where Lilly had died. The archbishop had led the service, followed by Bao, Jake, and Juliana telling their own stories of the life they had been blessed to share with Sarah and John over the years. Their headstones had been set with Lilly's in the grove. Simple. Their names together on a stone with Lilly, "In love they lived, together they will arise." Orchids again were set everywhere and given to friends as they left by the gatehouse. Little pots of the small red orchids Sarah surrounded herself with in her bath were given to friends as they left. Sarah's favorite gift was always to share their beauty and uniqueness. Like Sarah, there would never be two exactly alike. As far as any of them knew, this orchid was created by Sarah alone. No wonder Lizzie didn't recognize it. She asked Sarah's assistant if it had a name.

"Why yes," she said. "It's called Lilly's Venganza. Lilly's Revenge" in Spanish."

Red was for passion, for anger. Sarah had still been angry? She had never really forgotten, she just tried to turn it into something beautiful. Lizzie had other plans for Lilly's revenge and her anger at those who hurt little girls. She had not forgotten, and the world didn't seem to want her to.

After everyone had departed, Jason Hamlin, their family attorney, had asked if Lizzie had a few minutes for him. "Just something personal your mother requested I give to you myself when the time came." He and Bao would be meeting with her later that week to discuss the estate when she was ready. He understood she had many more things to think about other than business. "Not to worry, Lizzie, all is in good hands. Your father was an exceptional businessman; astutely he watched over it all, but his greatest gift was hiring the best people and letting them do their jobs. Can I see you at seven tonight before I leave for San Diego? If that is okay with you? Meet you in your dad's office, I mean… your office now," he had said looking at Lizzie for acknowledgment.

"Sure, Dad's office," replied Lizzie, not really wanting to talk to anyone, but she knew there were many things she would have to deal with eventually and a few minutes for something her mom thought important was acceptable.

It was dark, Lizzie's favorite time in the library. Her dad would have been at his desk finishing up the business of the day, Mom curled up in her favorite velvet rose chair, feet crossed on a tapestried footstool, book in hand, glasses down on the tip of her nose. The fire would be warming everything, lights low across the bookshelves, Juliana's girls coming in to say goodnight. Not this night. Never again. Jason Hamlin was sitting in a chair, cup of tea in hand, staring at the fire when Lizzie walked in. On her dad's desk sat a small box she had never seen before. Lizzie had not had much need for things of her own, but she had seen boxes like this before in antique stores. Chinese, carved with dragons flying over a river beside ragged mystical mountains, most likely camphor wood. Looked old. Excellent condition. Not her mom's style, however. Lizzie walked over and touched it. The smell of camphor wood, exotic, fragrant. It strangely affected her. She shivered. The air changed. A breeze? No, the windows were closed.

"I tried to dust it off. Looks like no one has touched it in a hundred years," said Jason. "It was your mom's, now I assume it's yours. She told me when she was gone to give it to you. I know nothing about it. There is a secret safe room here in the library where many documents and journals have been kept for generations. There are some photos and a jewelry safe your Mom kept the family heirlooms in there as well. Turns out that even though Sarah wasn't much into jewelry, her mother and John's mother had been. The box was on a shelf with those things. In the will it is specifically stated that I am to give this to you after the services, but before the will is read. Only your dad, mom, and I have had the key, plus the electronic codes to the vault. Now it is you and I if you wish, and I would assume you may want to include Bao in things at some point. Your parents considered him their adopted son. Over the years I have learned why. I have much regard for Bao."

He walked over to the bookshelves, moved a few books out of the way, inserted an old key into a lock and the bookshelf opened- up slowly. A solid metal door was behind that with an electronic keypad. He put in some numbers and handed her the key attached to a rabbit's foot.

"I know, odd. Your dad said it was easy to find, and the code is your great, great grandfather's birthday. It's always been in that family bible on the third shelf. Oh, on your dad's side of course. I know that's sort of crazy and I'm sure you will change it."

He tapped three times on the Chinese box in such a way Lizzie thought it just might open magically. "Here is a letter from your mom. They loved you and truly respected your work abroad. I will be here to help in any way that you may need assistance. Please, Lizzie, remember you are not alone. There are many people who love you and will help you in this difficult time. I've got a flight to catch. Let's talk soon dear girl. Be safe, Lizzie."

"Goodnight Jason, and thank you," wondering why he had said "be safe." She thought it odd he was catching a commercial flight, and then remembered all their planes were grounded for inspections. "Just to be safe" Chuck had said.

Jason shut the door behind him quietly. The window on the other side of the room blew open, and a real chill came over the room, Lizzie walked over and quickly latched it. She just couldn't let any more ghosts in that night. Of course, it was already too late for that.

Chapter 14

The Box—the Necklace

Lizzie put another log on the fire and poured herself a tall glass of water in one of her mom's Waterford goblets. Hers now, she thought. What an odd feeling. All of this had always been part of life, but not her life. Lizzie's grandparents' home, her family home, now Lizzie's, and she assumed Bao's home. She preferred the cabin and could not imagine moving back in here. Lizzie did love the library, the smell, the books, artifacts from the many places they had all gone together, the map of the world. Their world, her parents' world mostly, so she had always thought since leaving college and going abroad. Not to worry, Jake and Juliana will enjoy it.

Sitting down on the floor, leaning back on her mothers' rose chair in front of the fireplace; the ever-busy oriental carpet seemed the perfect spot to read Sarah's letter and open the mysterious box. Letter first, according to the notes on the envelope. She opened the letter, recognizing her mother's lovely cursive script immediately. No one wrote like that anymore. She could almost hear her mother's voice. See her holding her pen so perfectly. She leaned back on the seat of the chair, looked one more time into the fire, and then down at the lovely rice paper Sarah loved to use. Orchids embossed all around the edges.

Dear Lizzie,

> *If you are reading this, both your father and I are gone. Hopefully, we went close together, the idea of being apart would be too much for either of us. I hope someday you will find love like I have had. No relationship is ever perfect. We had our challenges. I never thought I could forgive him for*

hiring Gregor. I never thought I could heal from losing Lilly. But we go on, and we must forgive those we love. Life opens new doors, and working in my gardens, I witnessed the arrival of spring once again. I pray you will find your spring, your season.

I am sure you are feeling quite alone, but you have Bao, Jake, Juliana, and the girls. Please don't shut them out. I know a part of you died with Lilly. I had hoped you would find someone special; now as time has passed, I worry more, what weight Lilly's death truly had upon you. Bao told me what really happened. It will always be our secret. I would have done the same. But those kinds of things change us.

History repeats itself it seems. We all have secrets. In the box you will find many, I think. The box was given to me by my mother, and it was given to her by her mother, Granny Elizabeth. It has been passed down only to be opened by her namesake. So, it seems only you and Elizabeth will know what's in it. The rest of us honored the rule. Enclosed in the envelope is the key. Open the box. Maybe part of your story is in there. I wish you love, joy, and as you wish, adventure, my dear. Take care of our flowers. Fly high.

Love, forever and ever,
Mom

Lizzie put down the letter, took the key with the Chinese letters on it, and opened the box. It smelled old, but the smell of camphor cleared her head back to the present. Inside was a quilted baby blanket with birds, flowers, animals, and fish embroidered on it. There were several old black and white photos looking like the kind at the turn of the century. A woman holding a baby in this blanket by a dark river with canyon walls behind them. A portrait of the same woman up close with a gold necklace, the pendant, a dragon with ruby eyes holding a pearl in its claws. A photo of three young men. A leather journal with the initials M.B. on it. A skeleton key with a leather tag embossed "Jack" and the name "Bolder Hardware" on an old bronze key ring. A copy of the deed to "Bolder Hardware" was attached. Lizzie stood up in front of the fireplace, and in doing so caught a glimpse of herself in the mirror over the mantle. The face in the mirror was the same as the one in the portrait. Lizzie was sure she had never seen a picture of this woman and never heard of a "Bolder Hardware". But she was about to find out. She untied the leather journal, carefully, as it seemed fragile, the pages yellowed and a little ragged. The first line read "Be careful with your memories for they will be with you forever." Maddie Bolder, October 14, 1902. Boy, could Lizzie relate.

Chapter 15

The Great Escape

It was raining hard in Oakland that morning, almost like the Gods wanted to wash away any memory of the last few days. Sarah and John lay with Lilly in the family cemetery. Jason, Jake, Bao, and Lizzie had gone over the estate. Everything was in order as was to be expected, knowing John and Jason. Nothing needed to be done by Lizzie, right now, as most of her parent's assets passed over to her, overseen by Jason Hamlin and Bao, unless Lizzie chose differently. The ranch in Sao Paulo went to Juliana and Jake's family since their roots were there. John had felt that was best, knowing someday they would return to Brazil. Cookie and the staff were welcome to stay on to take care of the house, the gardens, the family, but were left a generous gift that allowed them to set up a life elsewhere if they so choose. Bao was left the cabin at the Lakehouse, stock in the companies and an inheritance that would take care of him till the end of his days. He would continue to work for Orchid, now as chief operating officer. He had worked with John at Orchid International and Genesis, with seats on both boards. He could have walked out the door that moment, an independently wealthy man, but of course, he did not. Lizzie's parents had included him in everything from the moment Lizzie was born and it would never change. Lizzie knew some things were deeper than blood. Secrets, that she now knew, Sarah had been privy to as well. Had her father too? Had John said something to Jason that led him to tell Lizzie to be safe? Were they concerned about her or what she was capable of? No, she just had let her mind run wild after reading her mom's letter.

Juliana and Jake were staying on here until the girls graduated high school now. Jake would step into John's shoes overseeing Genesis's vast holdings all over the world from Oakland but basing themselves back in Sao Paulo eventually. Bao would take over Orchid entirely. Sarah had started it, but it had been years since she had been involved in the financial side of things. She had preferred the quiet work in the greenhouses. Bao had amazing insight into Orchid and John always said he could see through the money and the personalities, knowing what, really, was about to transpire. Bao understood the cultural differences working in Southeast Asia and had learned a lot in Brazil from Jake. John had said Bao had no emotions when it came to business. He could understand why. Cambodia had taken all. Where he came from you needed to know where the tigers hid. Even in the world of orchids, there were lots of sleeping tigers.

Juliana had started a new Our Lady of Hope in Berkeley, and she was already in need of expansion. She had started a conversation with the young Reverend Andrew, the archbishop's assistant, at the brunch, after the services for John and Sarah, about a boarding school for aged-out foster kids, abandoned immigrant and trafficked children. Reverend Andrew had suggested the old Catholic school here in Berkeley he had trained in might work, with some adjustments. It had been vacant for many years. For that matter, the church itself had been emptying slowly. Only old folks came regularly anymore. Sure, they still did weddings and funerals. Christmas and Easter were always full. It would be good to see the campus full of people again.

Juliana said, "Most are still children, twelve to eighteen years old. Their souls wounded. Hearts broken. Bodies battered, some malnourished." The Reverend Andrew McGuire was aware of those poor lost souls he saw too frequently on the streets of the city these days. Juliana and Lizzie knew just where to get the souls from. The E.R. rooms, the churches that had free meals, the homeless camps were full of them. They walked the streets at night, too dangerous to sleep, and slept on buses and park benches during the days. With nowhere to go, they often just went back to their pimps or traffickers or started down that path. Deep in legal issues, not likely to be easily adopted or claimed, the lost teens were an opportunity to do something positive with their energies right now. Lizzie overheard them and seconded the idea immediately, trying not to show her true enthusiasm. A trust fund for Our Lady of Hope was started by Lizzie, with ten million dollars for renovations. Jake and Bao matched. Friends and associates of the family added substantially once they heard about it. Sex trafficking was a hot topic with Jeffrey Epstein in the news. Forty million dollars was a fair start for a small catholic boarding school for girls or as Juliana put it, "Our Ladies of Hope." Jason would start work on any legal issues that were sure to arise. This was different than Sao Paulo in so many ways. They would need a couple of full-time attorneys, just to get the kids in the program and out of the broken system. Here the girls and boys would be safe, nourished physically and spiritually. Educated and directed to a college or a trade for their future. Most would have the opportunity to go to college. There had never been a program like it in the States. Juliana had been successful in Sao Paulo with it, but there were not so many hurdles to get going in Sao Paulo. Just a more dangerous crowd to save. Or so she thought.

Since the twins were back in school, staff all caught up, business attended to, and Juliana's project launched, Lizzie knew she needed space and Bao could see it.

He knew her contract had been up with Highland hospital and she had not really seemed like she was interested in staying on any longer. She had not been there since the accident.

"Take the Pullman," Bao said.

"The Pullman—we still have Dad's train? Where is it?" asked Lizzie.

"It's on its way back to Oakland today with JJ. Your father was going to surprise your mom with a trip through the Sierras, then to Oregon and Washington after their return from San Diego. It is ready for you if you want it. I think it would be good for you," Bao said with a smile and a bit of jealousy. He could see something more was troubling her, and he knew her well enough that her answers usually came on the road. She would tell him eventually.

"Go! We can handle anything here for a few weeks." They could handle anything for however long, Lizzie was free to do whatever she wanted. He just needed to be able to stay in contact with her. He just didn't want to give her too much room, too much time. He knew she would take it all. "I'll call you if I need you. You still have that pink iPhone, right?"

"Never give it up! Great idea, I need some time to gather my thoughts, what I want to do next, what my place is in all this now. Dads Pullman, the mountains, I want to go to Oregon. Thank you, Bao, you always know what I need."

He didn't know what this new desire to go to Oregon was about. He knew after she had brought the Chinese box back to the cabin, she had started asking lots of questions and looking through all the family albums and photos she could find. She was looking for something, but since there was no one left in the family to ask…she had a need to go to Oregon. Not like he could stop her.

Lizzie packed a couple of worn Eddie Bauer jeans, boat shoes, hiking boots, rain boots, blue Ked sneakers, her fav light blue down jacket, thick wool socks, and red plaid flannel pajamas. It had been a long time since she had been to Oregon, but she remembered the nights could get cold quickly. She was going to the cabin in Oregon, and it took a while to get the woodstove going in there, as she recalled. "Yes, the cabin, would be good. Mom loved it there—she always talked about how it brought her such peace. She liked being in the high mountains, and the clear, star-filled skies made her feel closer to God and Lilly. Where there were no interruptions for your thoughts. That was before the Internet and cell phones." Oh well, thought Lizzie, I can pretend it's 1980 and turn them off. Easy enough. I will be on a train built in the 1920s and a cabin from the 1890s! Time can stand still. Nice thought anyway, she mused.

Bao took Lizzie to the train station, rain pouring down, splashing them both. He briefly boarded The Belle with her. Her Pullman now, it was just as she remembered it when they took it on the trip through California. Sarah and John's room was the same, overstuffed feather bed, bath with a copper shower, dark woods, oriental carpets made to fit precisely. The bunk room Lizzie had used was turned into a traveling greenhouse-library office with the bunks removed and her dad's books moved. Johns' favorite classics and Sarah's favorite botanicals and ancient medicine notebooks took over the area the top bunk had been. A full-length work area to spread out specimens, take the ever-flowing notes of Sarah's, a computer, and a color printer where the bottom bunk had been, underneath, two refrigerators with varying temperatures. Her parents' desire to learn was insatiable. It looked as if her mom was setting this up for research. There were some plant specimens and vials in the small refrigerator that she would check into later. She recognized the vial of devil's breath along with some other potentially lethal toxins and antidotes. Odd, but convenient for Lizzie. The trip was to go through the Sierras first, leaving with other private train cars on a jaunt. Somehow, they would switch over with Amtrak in the next week or so and head northwest to Oregon, stopping in at Bolder. Lizzie was curious—okay, more than curious—to see this Bolder Hardware. She had googled it. It was next to a museum now, The Bolder Hotel, run by a trust under the name Bolder Trust of course. In the hands of the city of Bolder for years, that trust had been set up a hundred years ago for its maintenance. Not enough to run it as a hotel it seemed, but seasonally enough to use as a museum. It apparently had quite a history to it. Tunnels, secrets, ghosts. She whispered to herself as she so often did these days. Maybe my ghosts are there.

JJ stepped into the sitting room where Lizzie and Bao were saying their goodbyes. "All aboard who are going aboard," he said with a great smile. Bao hugged her, kissed the top of her head, just like her dad used to, and jumped off the train waiving his A's baseball cap at her.

"Try and stay out of trouble, Lizzie—if you can," he said with a true look of concern in his black eyes. 'Whatever does he mean?' she wondered. For the first time since Bao had called about the crash, she breathed, really breathed, and the train engines roared to a start. "All aboard!" shouted JJ., a saying she associated with adventure and discovery. And with healing, she hoped.

Chapter 16

Into the Mountains

"Leaves falling reminds us that one must let go for new to come."

The high Sierras are beautiful any time of year, but fall is Lizzie's favorite season on the west coast. They left at dark from Oakland, while still raining, which was perfect. JJ made Lizzie some hot chocolate, just like she had back when she was ten. She had handed him the Arusha coffee upon arrival, for the mornings, but cocoa was just the ticket right then. After getting settled in, Lizzie put on her red plaid flannels, thick wool socks, got into bed, and opened a book of Mom's notes that she had left by her bed. It was a list of plant interactions—on the cover page was a drawing of the Borrachero tree; her dear friend, "Devils Trumpet." Serendipity strikes again. That lovely, very toxic plant outside in the garden at the ranch. Interesting! Lizzie wondered why Sarah was still curious about this white flower, after all those years? Had she noticed that some was missing from their lab? She read her mom's fine handwriting describing news reports of its use recently in Brazil. Excited, but mostly exhausted, Lizzie fell asleep to the rocking of the train, her dreams full of orchids and vines tangling everything around her. White and red buds growing out of her hands and feet…

Private train cars often go with a group of other Pullmans and that's what this was supposed to start out as, leaving Oakland. A fall tour of the Sierras attached to Amtrak. Ten privately owned Pullmans, each unique and beautifully refurbished. For the first few stops, Lizzie stayed on board; her photo had managed to stay out of the papers, but not her name. Mostly sleeping and reading, enjoying steamy hot showers. She did not want to mingle with anyone, but she suspected Bao would think it a good distraction if she did. He obviously hadn't known her as well as he thought. Her parents had enjoyed all of it. They had friends that also had kept up old family personal coaches. It was a very exclusive group. Not many folks had ever even seen one of these cars outside of a train museum, let alone live in one for a week or more. At five thousand dollars a day to rent, a rare treat indeed. Traveling in a group somehow managed to keep some anonymity. No one knew if you were renting or owned. They stopped briefly to do a local historical tour, to check out the local fare and wine tasting for those who wished, and then were back on the tracks in a few hours. A lovely thing about traveling by personal coach, there are no tickets, no one knows who is on the train when they get off or not, and no one bothers you. Especially if you have 3rd generation JJ on board to attend to all your needs. Lizzie felt like a princess. She knew this was part of her world and her parents would be glad she was using it, but a part of her was still in Africa, fighting for the albino children, another part wanting to kill those who throw away little girls, white, brown, or black. Her privilege, her parents taught her, came with a cost. She knew she could only be a princess for so long and then what? What was she?

As the miles went by through canyons, along rushing rivers, the steep granite mountains surrounding them, Lizzie counted the blessings her parents had afforded her. She had no idea what was next. The truth was, she had never worked for a living—she worked to save lives. Sooner or later, Lizzie needed to get back to work at something for her sanity. The corporate world was Jake and Bao's domain. Juliana had the girls, and now, Our Ladies of Hope, times two. She couldn't see going back to the E.R. for a while. It was too tempting to want to kill the garbage that walked through the doors every day. Lizzie wanted to get rid of them all, but she knew she couldn't. If she wanted to kill again it would have to be well thought out. If she listened to the voices in her head, there was a lot of work, planning, and preparation to be done for the next one. She could never do what she had done at Highland again. Everywhere she had traveled or lived, creeps crawled amongst the innocent. Lizzie was waking up to something she had felt whispering in her soul for a long time. She knew now Highland was only a start.

No one really knows me, she thought joyfully to herself. The papers list Lizzie as heir to the Orchid Group and a conglomerate of international pharmaceutical companies, Genesis. She was rumored to be an eccentric young woman who never leaves the house, which obviously had no truth to it at all. Her family had over-protected her after Lilly's murder, she was rarely alone until she went to college. And then she learned to like her privacy so much that she had requested her parents honor it even more so and to please ask first before including her in parties. She had thus avoided being in her parents' social crowd despite their hopes and wishes she'd mingle a little bit. When traveling abroad, Lizzie blended right in with the other docs and nurses. She rarely wore anything new and kept few personal possessions. That was also normal for contract people. Gypsies don't travel with much. Stuff just got in the way.

How things have changed, she thought, as she sat in her sitting room by the fire-lit logs in her private coach. It looked so real, but Dad had changed it to gas, due to rules and regulations that Amtrak had these days. Still, 'it felt warm and good, surrounded by books, ferns, and orchids. How JJ managed it all was beyond her. Cookie and Joy must have told him what she liked to eat it was all there if she got hungry They had wireless now too. Lizzie read her mom's notes and books. She slept a lot. She would take walks whenever the train stopped, sure to get off before others departed and back on before they returned. More than anything, Lizzie craved her privacy right now. JJ was literally a ghost on the train, only there when she rang. He basically lived in the kitchen, a bunk and small bathroom on the other side. He always stayed with the train when it was on the tracks, giving her a heads up when to return. Soon, they would head towards Oregon and she wanted to be rested when she went to discover the Bolder Hardware store and particularly the hotel. The Chinese dragon box and its contents were stored in her room under the bed, locked, the key on a leather cord around her neck. Bao was right about one thing: she did need time to think. As the days went by, they finally headed through the canyons along the Sacramento River and up through Dunsmuir, a wonderful old railroad town. They parked a day there, visiting a railroad museum and walking up the Castle Crags. Lizzie's mom had told her about this area and how her family had logging companies near here, east of McCloud and west of Weed, up north through Oregon. She had told Lizzie that The Hearst family had built a fairy castle named "Wyntoon" near here, on the McCloud river, but few had ever seen it, since it had been kept in the family for generations and only visible from the river. Lizzie remembered their fun trip to San Simeon and could only imagine what the castle in the woods was like. Sarah had been invited there once on her way to Oregon and it was quite magical, but somewhat haunted with all its stories of family rivalries and romances.

They rounded Mt. Shasta, beautifully feather dusted with the first snow of the season. Lizzie remembered hearing about this magical mystery mountain. Her mother loved to tell stories about the Indian lore between Mt Shasta and Mt Mazama, now known as Crater Lake. It seemed like Lizzie was entering another world here as she crossed the Oregon border and her mother's stories started coming back. Maybe she might find something to direct her to the next chapter of her life, on this road to Oregon. God surely knew she needed direction. She wished on a star in those big open night skies that first night crossing the border. It was barely light when they pulled into Bolder. JJ had arranged a spur and a train shed for them for a week, or however long it was supposed to take for her to check things out. She really had no idea how much time she needed here. Yet. This was a major railyard for the west coast, and they could hide out in one of the storage barns for a while. Some might be curious, but JJ could handle it. Custom repairs being done or some such thing. As soon as the train stopped, Lizzie jumped off, heading for Main Street. The train station in Bolder was just the same as she had seen in photos in the box. Lizzie googled the Bolder Hotel Museum, noted it was about a mile away, and set off on foot towards Main Street.

At 6 a.m., Main Street was foggy, a mist known to come in every morning in these parts due to the surrounding tules and long shallow lake. The shadows coming from the streetlights with the mist swirling in and out, made it look like ghosts slowly strolling down the sidewalks.

Lizzie felt like she could almost see them walking, skirts swishing, walking sticks clicking on the sideboards, laughter, and chatter as they moved... There were still many of the original buildings from the turn of the century. Some turned into law offices, dress shops, several original bank buildings from 1901, beer pubs, and coffee houses. She had read there was the only elevator in Oregon, with an elevator attendant, in the tallest building in town. She would have to come back and see what that was about. At six stories it was the tallest building downtown. At one time, The Bolder Hotel had been the tallest. It was the first hotel for the town and had been owned by a family named Bolder, of course. Now it had been set aside for a museum. Lizzie had a key that would hopefully unlock some of the mystery around all of this. A key that went where? Before contacting the curator of the museum, she wanted to look around herself. She did still own the hardware store after all, and in an odd kind of way, she owned the hotel as well, since the ground was held in a family trust. She only had a key to the hardware building though, it seemed. A random skeleton key, more like something that would go to an old jail cell it seemed. The building looked deserted, dirty windows partially boarded up. The leaded glass windows up high still amazingly intact, the paint on the heavy double doors, chipped from many years of weather, but solid still.

She stood there looking it over. It lay at the end of Main Street. The old hotel and hardware store sat by a wide, dark, slow-moving river, a parking lot above it on the hill, some red oak trees planted in front. A big park across the street for Veterans now had been the site of a huge timber mill at one time. She tried to imagine what it really looked like before paved roads. Before cars—it was old enough. Walking to the front doors, she looked for a place for a skeleton key to go. All the locks had been changed over and there were alarms, or so it said with the stickers in the windows, Bolder Security Systems. She went around the side by the river, where the original rock foundation still stood, windows with iron grids and an old steel door to the basement. A large original skeleton key lockset was here. Dusting it off with her jacket and then blowing the cobwebs out, she slid the key in. Rusty, but

111

it fit. She turned the key. No handle on the outside, the door hinges and lock rusted. When was the last time somebody opened this, she thought? She took her red Swiss army pocketknife out, Chuck had given her a thousand years ago, scraping along the edge of the door, it cracked open a hair. No alarms here. She used the knife to scrape some more, and the door pushed inwards. Turning on her phone flashlight, she could see another door a few feet in. Thick dust on the floor and more spider webs, no one had been here for a century it seemed! The key worked here too. Two locks, one key? She stepped inside. Time stopped here. She smelled it. Old book smell, with cigars? Reminded her of the basement at the Lakehouse and something else she couldn't quite remember. But it made her skin crawl.

Last night, Lizzie had reviewed the diary again, of Maddie Bolder, in anticipation of what she would find? She wanted to understand more before she unlocked that second door.

The journal spanned a lifetime, 1890 to the day before she died in 1916—the day Maddie slipped into the cold, dark water of that river next to the hotel for the very last time. Maddie wrote how she had loved that river—the rippling waters that usually calmed her soul and some days tormented her—the river that eventually she gave her life to.

Until Maddie was 12, life was fun—lots of guests at the hotel and summers with her grandmother at their summer cabin at Lost Horse Lake. She loved that time, especially if the boys were off with her father. They were generally tolerable, but they had made some older male friends up from the city and her brothers were picking up their bad habits. They teased her and often tried to get her alone. She knew enough to know that was not a good idea. She stayed busy and out of their way as much as possible. One night she was down in the basement getting some jams and jellies from the kitchen and she heard the boys laughing and saw the door to Father's "smoke" room open slightly. She tried to be quiet but as she turned to go up the stairs, one of the boys, Jack, grabbed her arm. He smelled of whisky, calling her miss prissy, "Too good for us, are you? Come in and have a drink with us, Maddie." He pushed her through the door and onto the floor, closing the door behind him, then locking it. The boys were drunk, eyes glazed over, sprawled over her father's big old wing chairs. Maddie yelled at them to let her out, they just laughed and rolled their eyes. Since her father's smoke room was in the basement, it was surrounded by rock, basically, an underground cave dug inside the hillside. Perfect for cigars, scotch and the man talk Mother despised. Not for ladies. They wouldn't have to hear them "cussing" she would say to Maddie. No one could hear her screams that's for sure. Still, Jack put his hand over her mouth, pushed her down on the small bed they kept for nights when one of them had to sleep off a drunk. He tossed her dress over her head and raped her right in front of her brothers. They just watched and laughed. After he was finished, Jack ripped the necklace her father had given her with the dragon and pearl from her throat and swore he would kill anyone who told what happened here. Her brothers were worse cowards than she had imagined but Maddie never thought they were this bad. She escaped to her room crying. She took what was left of her dress off. It was bloody and torn. She hurt horribly. What would she tell her mother? She could not tell her mother or father. What would they do? They had told her to stay away from the boys. They would blame her. Jack would kill her. The boys would be off to college soon and she would be safe finally, right? She would find a way to get away from here. She would steer clear as possible from them. Somehow.

Years later, in her journal, Maddie talks about the young men her parents introduced to her. For some reason she seemed to have no interest, discouraging all. She wanted to go to college too, but Father had said, "No, girls don't need college, they needed a good husband." He did however let her learn photography, mostly to do work for the hotel, for the hardware ads, and friends' portraits, but she took to it so well that soon the newspapers were hounding her for her work. She took pictures of everything, both the dark side of the city and the light-hearted. There was plenty of fodder. Maddie had an exceptional eye for the unusual, the exotic, the curiosities. When her brothers invited Jack back one summer, they had asked for her to take a picture of the three of them together with the river in the background. Had they completely forgotten what had happened? Jack had brought his new bride along. Did she know who he really was? He was staring at Maddie in a way that gave her chills. Of course, she hated him. Jack made a comment about how she had filled out and whispered that he would like to give it a go again with her. Like she had enjoyed the last time. "More experienced now, I'm sure," he said. Maddie pleaded with Mother to let her go to the cabin at Lost Horse Lake, telling her she had been invited by friends to join in a hike to the mountain lakes. Maddie had gone by herself before to the cabin. She loved it there, always quiet, the cool waters of the Lost Horse Lake, swimming under brilliant blue skies. It was her piece of heaven. No bad memories there. Maddie thought there would be nothing to attract the guys either. They liked town, the saloons, the card houses, the showgirls. The "ladies of the night." Her mother and father just acted like that's what boys did. Father went with them sometimes. The boys rarely came back with him though. Maddie knew what that usually meant. She was just relieved they were staying away from her when they did that, but with Jack in town, she needed out.

Her mother finally agreed after Maddie had pleaded all that day, agreeing to take on several more jobs for her mother upon her return from the cabin. She would go by ferry and then a short hike to the cabin. Maddie knew the area well and everyone up there had known her since she was a young girl. She took her old hound dog, Blue, with her. What she hadn't known was that her brothers had told Jack where she had gone. He came for her the next night, while she was sleeping. She woke to hear Blue barking, then a gunshot, then silence. Maddie couldn't move fast enough. By the time she had gone for her rifle over the door he was in the house and had his gun pointed at her, told her to sit in the chair, he had something he wanted to talk to her about. He stepped behind her and then struck her head with the barrel of his rifle. She woke up tied to the bed, gagged. He told her if she kicked, he would shoot her. He proceeded to rape her several times the rest of the night. When he was finally done with her, he untied her, and he hit her one more time for good measure. She hurt like hell, she was dizzy, the warm, sticky blood dripped down her face, she closed her eyes, tasting her own blood, and pretended to be dead. Jack had been drinking all night. When he left, he didn't know if she was dead or not. He didn't care. But she wasn't dead. No one was looking for her to return for a week. She told her hiking friends she had fallen ill and would miss the hike. She came home bruised and said she had fallen off the ladder to the loft. Nine months later she had a baby. Jack's baby. Keeping the pregnancy hidden wasn't difficult. No one paid that much attention to a 26-year-old "old maid." She just wore looser clothes. Her mother told her she was getting fat. Her father gave her cookies. Maddie kept quiet.

Maddie knew a woman at her church, Annie Logan, who prayed constantly for a baby. Maddie knew what to do with that baby when the time came. She shared with Annie her predicament, just saying the man had lied to her, was going to marry her, but had run off when hearing she was pregnant. Annie and her maid helped with the delivery. Maddie, a few days later, left Annie's house, leaving the baby in Annie's arms, wrapped in a lovely, embroidered blanket, with Elizabeth stitched on the edge. A name Annie picked. Maddie put her journal, the photos, and a letter all in an oriental box and gave it to Annie. Someday someone will know the story, but for a long time, she must protect the sweet baby Elizabeth.

Lizzie now knew that baby was her great, great, Grandmother Elizabeth, her mother—Maddie Bolder. The baby's new mother was Annie Logan. The baby was known as Elizabeth Logan. Elizabeth had her grandmother, also named Elizabeth, who married John Ferry. John's daughter, Sarah, married John Harmen, Lizzie's father. If anyone else had ever read the journal or opened the box, Lizzie didn't know. She looked at the photo of the boys—read the back, and one was named Jack.

Lizzie thought to herself. I am a child of rape. Even if it was a hundred years ago, it whispered to her with its evil breath over the ages. Will it ever end? Maybe with me, thought Lizzie. Maybe with me. Maddie will be avenged somehow. As will my sweet, Lilly.

Chapter 17

Fall in Bolder

Bolder turned out to be a much more "interesting" place than she expected, so Lizzie had decided to stay awhile and take a job at the local E.R. She sent Jerry and the Pullman back after just four days. Fall was wonderful, full of color and the crisp mornings were perfect for Lizzie to wander around trying to retrace Maddie's life. Bolder was close to Lost Horse Lake, a place Lizzie had always wanted to go to since hearing her mom's stories. As it turned out, so had Maddie Bolder, until Jack tried to kill her there. Lizzie connected with Maddie and wanted to make things right for her, somehow, in some way. After Maddie had left the baby girl to her new mother, Annie, she had drowned herself in the partially frozen river next to the hotel. It was months before anyone found her. That winter, it was so cold she sank fast and deep. The town's people, who liked Maddie, hoped she had finally found her man and escaped the servitude of her now aging parents. She had always seemed like such an independent girl, but girls didn't leave their parents back then unless they married. They were not surprised when her body was found, just at a loss as who would care for them, they never believed she would just leave them. Their sons had turned out to be selfish boys who turned into self-absorbed men. They had used their family money to open doors and left long ago for San Francisco. Maddie had been a rock for them these past years. The museum had a lot of stories written by Maddie Bolder, amazing photographs of the area, and famous people that had come through that she had photographed. The local newspaper said she drowned, that she must have fallen through the ice. Annie knew different. Maddie had known that river and its inherent dangers like the back of her hand. She had given up her baby and then her own life.

"Local photographer, Maddie Bolder, found on the shores of Bolder Lake, missing since last December, drowned." Only Annie Logan guessed the truth. She left the area shortly after, returning to her family home in Oakland, California. She would return to Lost Horse Lake every summer, but avoid Bolder as much as possible, only taking Elizabeth many years later. Little Elizabeth never knew anyone else but the Logan family. The story of Maddie Bolder had stayed sealed until Lizzie had opened it just weeks ago. Her namesakes had preferred it so.

Enjoying the high desert mountains, surrounding forests, lakes, and the small town, Lizzie signed a three-month contract and bought a used, but well-maintained blue Jeep. She never bought new. Too conspicuous. She parked it two blocks from the train. She stayed on the train for the first few nights, checking things out and visiting the museum after dark or early mornings, when it was most likely no one was around. She loved being inside. Using her skeleton key, she could read Maddie's journals in the smoke room or wander the old hotel by flashlight. Sometimes the curator would leave the lights on, so no one thought it unusual if they saw a light. She was already inside, the old metal door on the side street to the hardware store, her main entrance, and the other secret door in the basement was her access to the museum basement, then upstairs. The alarms didn't go off since she was already in the building, leaving her free to roam as she wished. It was fun to imagine she was Maddie living in these rooms. There were pictures of Maddie and photographs taken by her everywhere. There were clothes from the 20s that she dared to try on. Weird, how they fit perfectly. Maddie had been small too. People used to be much smaller at the turn of the century. Were these Maddie's things? The old photos showed her in similar dress. The shoes were ridiculously too small, however, and horribly uncomfortable. She walked barefoot into a dusty bathroom, turned on the tub fixture, and miraculously it worked. She washed her feet off and slipped her shoes back on. The museum was closed during the winter months, for tourists, but the free geothermal heat kept it warm. Rarely did anyone but the curator come in. When Niles, the curator, arrived a few weeks later to prepare for a special event, he observed footprints by the tub. Odd he thought, the janitor must be cleaning barefoot? No these were small feet, a girl's feet. Maybe the place really was haunted by Maddie Bolder! He left the footprints there for "effect" for his next tour date.

Lizzie had a deep old clawfoot tub of her own in her new "turn-of-the-century" apartment, so that evening at home she filled the tub, let the water rise to her chin, and tried to imagine she was Maddie before the bad things happened. She had noticed, reading the other journals, there had been happy times before the boys became teens. Lizzie had loved sneaking into the museum to learn more about Maddie, but soon the museum season would be open, and she would have to discontinue her nocturnal haunts. Even with a key, she would have a lot of explaining to do. And that was a story she would have trouble explaining.

The hospital, though modern, was a hospital in a large agricultural community. With the field, came farmworkers, with them came illegals, and with them traffickers, but it surely wasn't exclusive to them. She had not seen any sex trafficking victims here yet, but on her second shift, she did get a white five-year-old girl, who, after examination, was positive had been mentally and sexually abused. Lizzie asked the mom what had happened? Had a stranger been in the house? Did she tell you what happened to her? Typical answer when asked of the mom what happened. "I don't know, I was working, she must have fallen…." The teenage boy with the earring in his eyebrow, dark shadows under his angry eyes, looked at Lizzie, stared at the floor, and shook his head, no. The mom did not see their secret exchange. Lizzie walked away, then stopped when she heard the two arguing.

"Your Jimmy did this to her, you know it, tell them!" he yelled.

"Shut up Ben, he will leave us! We have no money. Let them take care of her and then we will talk. Give me some time to think," she said.

"I hate him! I hate you! I'm going to kill him! He will never touch her again," Lizzie heard him spit at her. He had a look of a child who knew what had happened to his little sister because it had happened to him. He was just too old now for Jimmy. Lizzie didn't want him to ruin his life and kill Jimmy. And he'd be the first one they would come looking for.

Later that night when everyone was gone Lizzie looked the file over. Jimmy Bien, stepfather. Later Lizzie did a background check. Charges filed for beating both the mom and the boy. Dropped. Reported for sexual abuse of a teen boy five years ago in another state. He did time. On probation. Last address, 212 Oak St. She walked by there every day on her way to work. Nice enough street. Tree-lined. Middle class mostly. A mile from a park where lots of kids played. Young kids. Maybe she could entice him. She could look like a preteen if she wanted to. No makeup, baseball cap, 5 ft tall. Scrawny. Blue tennis shoes. Big eyes. He had never seen her, but she saw his photo. She could spot him.

Lizzie's mind drifted. Lizzie knew how well Devil's Trumpet could work. She thought of Highland Hospital and the man with the little bull tattoo. It is getting cold out now, and she thought about what she had read about cold water drownings. In the cold, they stay down long enough for most drugs to be out of the system. She had grabbed the Devil's Trumpet vials Sarah had brought on the train before JJ left and put them in her small refrigerator in the apartment. Excited by the idea of eliminating another problem, she absolutely knew she had a target. When she went in the next day, the little girl was in critical care, unconscious—internal bleeding they said. She would have to go to OHSU to the pediatric hospital. She had more damage than they could deal with here. Lizzie had no doubt she would instill permanent damage of her own and soon. She overheard the staff talking about the child. This had not been the first time they had seen this family in with questionable injuries. They hoped DHS would be called in this time. OHSU would have to call that one. The mom wasn't talking. But Lizzie had heard enough.

Bolder Newspaper, third page in, several months later. "Jimmy Bien, local businessman missing since fall, found in Bolder lake, investigation pending," Lizzie overheard a staff member in the lunchroom reading the news. He said, "Saw that family too often in here, they are better off without him, maybe somebody got smart and killed the creep." Lizzie thought to herself, maybe. Yes, Jimmy had gone to hell with her assistance. Devil's Trumpet worked well on him. Blew him back to the gates he had spawned out of. She just wished he would have stayed down longer.

Chapter 18

Did They Just Drown?

After Lizzie had watched Jimmy float away and slowly sink into the dark current, it seemed appropriate to spend the rest of the evening in Maddie's father's smoking room, just around the corner from the park. There were some dusty but comfortable leather high-back chairs and a small feather bed when she went in the first time. Spiders and mice had nested in the feather bed, so she hauled that out across the street and down the vacant hill one evening shaking it out, feathers blowing everywhere. The mice and birds would make short work of it for their new nests that winter. The chairs were salvageable and after a bit of cleaning up, she had made it her own "Lizzie den." She liked to go there occasionally and think about Maddie. There was a window with bars on it which she opened just a tad—enough to get some air in. There was no one on this side of the building facing the river, to notice a small light from her phone or the candles she liked to light. Someone would have to be walking around the museum, through the bushes, weeds, and rocks, to get to the iron door. One hundred years ago, according to Maddie's journal, there had been a dirt trail up to it, but the boys and Maddie's father had used the basement access through the hotel with the secret door from the hardware store. This side door was rarely used. Probably for deliveries of illegal booze and whores for her brothers. Looking where the feather bed had been, Lizzie tried to get the image of Maddie and Jack out of her mind. Maddie had detested her brothers. They continued to torment her, but never actually came after her, and she stayed as far from them and their friends as possible. They didn't hang around much anyway, busy with "errands" for their father. The business of wheeling and dealing tools and such. Mostly hanging out downtown at card houses and saloons. Lizzie's childhood had been so much different than Maddie's. Except for the creepy gardener Gregor, and Lilly's murder, Lizzie had been surrounded by people who cared about her. Still, losing one's twin in such a horrendous manner and living with the guilt had created a part of her that had to get even.

Lizzie felt relieved—in fact, she felt better than she had in months. The first kill of the little bull pimp was almost spontaneous. Getting rid of Jimmy, felt—well, inspiring. Planning his demise, poisoning him, ridding the universe of another pervert, getting rid of these "Jacks," seemed like her calling. She knew it was murder. What a story that would be. Heiress to Orchid International murderess, kills pedophiles. The story of Lilly dragged up again. No, she would not let that happen. She would be extremely careful. Untraceable poisons. Cold, deep waters. Wicked humans, no one would miss. Everywhere she had worked she had seen the sinful prey on the weak; children and women who had no one to protect them. Lizzie might not be able to protect all, but she could eliminate some. She would wait and see how things went with this one. Six weeks went by and the paper reported the body. The family acknowledged him but refused to claim him. She had done society a service. She had done well. Two down. But how many to go?

That spring three more male bodies were found, all in the water, no signs of foul play either. Considered accidental drownings. One in a lake, the other two in the river. One up-river, one downstream. No apparent connection to each other. Except Lizzie knew them. She had seen them at the hospital, heard stories from staff, or read about them in the paper. Each had one thing in common: They had sexually abused at least one child, or a woman, and had gotten away with it once and were under suspicion of others. Jimmy was about to be pulled in when his stepdaughter died, all assumed he was a suicide. The others were considered no great losses, no one identified them, and the police just closed those cases quickly. Bad guys usually end up in bad places, they liked to say. Lizzie figured she was just saving the taxpayers' money and keeping society a little bit safer. But it was getting time to go—too many bodies floating up around Bolder.

Early one morning she had found a black cat sleeping outside "Lizzie's den." Not thinking it had a home, she impulsively thought it might be a good idea to have a mouser for the day, so she let it in. Although she had rented a small studio apartment downtown after taking the job at the hospital, she enjoyed walking over to the Bolder museum after her shift, sometimes staying there until dawn. There had been a light rain-snow flurry the next morning and when Lizzie stepped outside, she could hear someone calling "Toby? Toby kitty? Kitty, kitty?" Just then "black cat" ran out the door. Lizzie closed it quickly and locked it, walking after the cat up the hill. As she rounded the corner, a tall red-headed woman stood there, startled to see Lizzie, but she obviously knew the cat, since he jumped right up in her arms. They both said "Hello" at the same time. Lizzie had seen the redhead before. She had seen her at the pub she went to occasionally with workmates and heard her joke with one of the nurses. Red-headed lady sheriff. She didn't think the gal noticed her though. Hopefully not, she tried to blend in. The redhead said, "I have been looking for this mouser for days. He is a rascal, a known transient, but a good mouser. I live in the old seven gables carriage house. You know, the one painted purple? We are planning on changing it some time, I just bought it that way. Do you live around here? I'm known around here as Sheriff Sandy Curly Fox."

"Yes, I live just down the road a bit," answered Lizzie, not giving her a name or place. "I just like to walk around when it's quiet like this. Well, usually quiet, you gave me a start too! Umm, have a good night, I mean good day," said Lizzie, as she walked away from the tall red-headed sheriff. She had a funny feeling. She liked her. Then again people like Lizzie probably shouldn't be going around getting close with the locals, let alone the police. Thank goodness it was getting to the end of her contract, all she needed was people starting to recognize her. She walked back the way she came, covering her tracks so as not to look like she had come from the old iron door. And then down the hill around the museum and back to Main Street. A few drunks were looking for places to lay their heads; wet and cold today, they should find shelter soon. A surprise spring snow blowing. They generally headed to the warming station when it got like this. She better hurry and get back to the studio; she had left her coat in the den. Now she would be freezing too for few blocks. She hurried back to the studio over the local martini bar, passing a few cars folks had left behind from the night before, smart enough to take a taxi, she hoped. As she tucked herself in, her last thoughts were of the tall redhead sheriff lady.

Now she remembered. She had seen her another time; she had escorted a prisoner into ER with a gunshot wound a week ago. No wonder she liked her. They were both crime fighters.

The sheriff got to lock them up. Lizzie got to get rid of them.

Chapter 19

Officer Sandy Curly Fox

Sandy Curly Fox felt something too when she met Lizzie. She instantly liked her, but the cop in her said something was not quite right. She hadn't said her name or where she lived. Two women at 5 a.m., one looking for her cat, the other one doing what? Walking vacant hillsides behind museums in the freezing cold? Sandy didn't recall her having a coat on. She did not look homeless, but you never know these days. She wasn't high and usually, those were the folks you met in the mid-hours. Curious indeed. She could hear Gramma G. saying, "Sandy, nothing good happening between midnight and dawn. You be home girl." Sandy would have to keep an eye out for her. Small town, sure to run into her again. She kind of looked familiar.

Sandy Curly Fox, three quarters Modoc Indian, a quarter Irish, tall and strong. She usually shows up with her red-blond ringlets sticking out of her baseball cap, her easily tanned skin, and piercingly dark, almost black eyes, burning through you. A testament to her Indian heritage. People don't always know what to think. That worked in her favor. A unique look, a bit disarming. Not a little gal either, like the brunette Sandy had just run into. That one almost looked like a teenager. There was nothing fragile or little girl about Sandy Curly Fox. She looked like she could kick your butt, and she would. Black belt and fire were what her Sensei would say about her before each competition back in college.

She had grown up on the reservation outside town with her Gramma G. Her father had left shortly after she was born, and her mother died in a car crash a year later. Her mother had stayed sober while the father was there and during the pregnancy, but after he left, her mom went back to drinking and drugs. Sandy was a healthy little girl,

125

a strong spirit, and wily enough to get nicknamed Curly Fox, thus Sandy Curly Fox. At ten, the older girls started harassing her and one day they got her down in the school locker room and cut those red locks off. She asked Gramma G. to dye her hair black like the other girls. Gramma G. refused. Instead, she sent her to the Bay Area to a catholic private school for girls. The night before she left, Sandy managed to "trim" the hair off one of the girls who had done the same to her. She found her passed out stoned in the old barn the kids hung out at and saw it as a great opportunity to get even. After a phone call "warning for Curly Fox" from one of her lady friends, Gramma G. had her in the Caddy and on the bus out of town before anyone woke the next day. Casino money came in very handy, and Gramma learned long ago to save it for a rainy day. That rainy day had come. School didn't come cheap, but between Gramma G., tribal scholarships, and her check from the casino, they made it work. It was a small tribe that was left, but good management had really helped set some of them up for a better future. Programs for health and education had been made available. Not all the reservations were like that or the casinos. Honestly, few managed their money around town like Gramma G., Indian or white. They could all learn a thing or two from G.

Sandy C. Fox entered Bentley, a private school in Oakland, with a short cut of curly red hair and a great forever tan as far as anyone knew. In a year it was long and curly again. Gramma G. thought it best she stayed there all year, of course coming home for holidays occasionally, and summers going on trips abroad with other classmates. It was amazing how many girls traveled in the summer too. There was art, history, and language studies abroad and camps to go to. Seemed their parents were busy elsewhere. Sandy just lied and said the same thing the other girls said. Parents were too busy doing their own thing. It didn't take long to figure out, that where she came from, might not be the story to tell there. So, she made one up, one that fit, one that none of the other girls questioned. Especially the ones who stayed behind as well. Here she was just that Irish girl who tanned well. Even ended up with a few freckles. She played lacrosse, volleyball, soccer, and despite being tall, never took to basketball. What she did like was karate and by the time she graduated she had achieved her Black belt and her 2nd level of Dan. She would train for the rest of her life. She never used it lightly, but now she had a sense of confidence that could carry her anywhere. Someday, she would visit the reservation again, but she would be a different person. A strong woman, a much wiser one. She was not embarrassed by her heritage anymore. Indian or Irish, both had strong, proud histories she had learned about at school. Her grandmother had raised her the best she could and was a respected elder in her tribe. She was not a girl that snuck around cutting stoned people's hair anymore. The name, Fox, now referred to her quickness to learn and ability to outwit her opponents. Sandy graduated top of her class, went home briefly, just long enough to review life on the reservation. So many kids that she knew growing up had died of drugs and alcoholism. Diabetes was running rampant in the Indian community now too. Although the circumstances of her exodus were odd, few really remembered her, other than as the little Indian girl with red hair and that she was "different" and had been made to go to school off the "res." Most were surprised she came back. Kids that left rarely came back. Sandy loved Gramma G. and they had talked often while she was at school. Sandy had got them both iPhones. She had worked part-time after school and on weekends at the Karate school just to make some extra money. They loved to facetime each other and send photos. Gram was not doing well that summer and it was time for Sandy to go home if only to say goodbye. Things had not improved as much as they should have for the Indian community despite the money from the casino. Sandy didn't know the answer, however, she wanted to help somehow. She spent a month with Gramma G. The locals were friendly, but some of the kids she grew up thinking she was kind of snooty and accused her of acting better than them, so she and Gram stayed to themselves mostly. Gramma G. just reminded her they were jealous and too afraid to make something new of themselves. Still Sandy knew what it was like. She had been one of them for a while and counted her blessings that Gramma G. had the wisdom to get her a way out. Still, she felt like she needed to do something to help them. She knew it wasn't right to just take the scholarships and casino money. She couldn't just leave like some from the tribe had done after college. It was her turn to make a change.

They had that time between high school and college for Gramma to tell her the stories of old times, showing her the plants that some still used for medicinal purposes, and sharing the secret hunting and fishing spots her people had somehow managed to hide from the white man. The tribe didn't completely accept her, but nor did they reject her, as few these days were full-blooded Indians. The three local tribes had blended over the years and many had married outside the tribe altogether. Gramma G. told her the story again of how she came to her name. As a child, Gramma had the annoying way of popping up everywhere, at any time, to her parent's displeasure. Over the years she still made a point of popping up in people's business which was expected of such a respected elder. Gramma G. stood for Gramma Gopher.

All Gramma G had left was Sandy now. Like many elders in the tribe, they raised their grandchildren. Many had lost their grown children. Sandy's mom was one of them. Everybody said it was a car crash. Sandy had heard her mom used drugs and drank a lot. For that reason alone, Sandy might have chosen not to drink. Being Irish too, nailed that door shut for her. Not worth the risk. Karate had taught her about self-discipline. From what she had seen on the "res" and at her preppy school, alcohol didn't do that much for anyone. She had cleaned up after her cousins when she was ten and she had held a roommate's hair over the toilet while the girl threw up half the night from a party involving tequila and ecstasy. No, that was not for Sandy.

Gramma Gopher died peacefully in her sleep one night, in her favorite old blue ratty recliner chair. Sandy not wanting to disturb her went to put a quilt she had helped make a thousand years ago, over her. When she touched her hand to see if she might wake, it was cold and fell off the sidearm, just hanging there. She nudged her a little and Gramma Gopher did not pop up. She had outlived her children, her husbands, and many of her people. She had helped many to make better decisions for their lives. Another reason why Sandy had never drunk alcohol was that she knew her Gramma went to the Al-anon meetings and sometimes took her along. She took anyone and everyone to those meetings. There wasn't one person she knew who wasn't affected by someone's drinking or that had lost somebody too young in a drunk driving car accident. Gramma was one of the last elders who remembered the old ways. But she was not the last sober one. She had helped many. Today there were many clean and sober Indians, and they are taking that same energy of getting in trouble, into improving the life of the tribe. Gramma G started many of those sobriety circles. Sandy only found out that summer, that when she was in school, Gramma G was busy in her sobriety circles, helping others all those years.

Sandy was glad she had come home. She wrote down the stories Gramma G told her, as best she could recall. She boxed up the family heirlooms of baskets, pottery, and beadwork that had been in their family forever. Drawings from the Jackson boys, artists in the clan who had made it in the outside art circles across the country, were cherished. Sandy would have them in her home someday when she had one with walls of her own to nail things up. For now, she would store them somewhere safe.

For the time being, though, she headed to the southwest, to the University of Arizona in Tucson. They had a great American Indian studies program and Sandy wanted to study Tribal Law, history, and tribal women's issues. One of the big things she noticed was how poorly the women were treated on the reservation still. If somebody got beat, it was just the way it was. The police didn't come. The tribal police just told them to settle down. Women had disappeared on the "res" and nothing was ever done. No one went looking. Men would say they must have just runoff. One would hope they had the sense too. But with little education and no money, where would they go? Sandy wanted to make a difference. Her professors wanted her to go work for the Bureau of Indian Affairs. She tried for a while, but it wasn't enough for her. She craved interaction with the people and hated the bureaucracy.

There was one case that just broke her heart. The mother of a ten-year-old Indian girl, Tiny Bear, named because, although small, she was ferocious. The girl had been raped. They wanted justice. The girl had been found near a creek, half her body still in the shallow water. She had crawled out barely alive. Hikers had found her, just outside of the "res." Some teenage boys had taken her for a ride, each had raped her, beat her, tossed her in the creek, and left her for dead. She wasn't. The hikers called the police. They were not on the "res," so the local sheriff came out. He immediately called Life Flight and a Koala helicopter was there in fifteen minutes. At the hospital, she told the police who had done this to her. It was her cousins. She named them. Sandy was the prosecuting attorney. The tribe went quiet. These boys had been trouble. The boys were under eighteen, and, being the crime was on federal land, they did time at a juvenile prison for boys. One of the boys hung himself while there. Some members of the tribe thought Sandy, being Indian herself, should have done more to keep them out of jail. Tiny Bear was damaged forever, both spiritually and physically, and inside the tribe, no one would have anything to do with her. She was not welcome on the "res" anymore. Indians were not supposed to report Indians. Sandy was able to find assistance to get both mother and Tiny Bear a place in another town. They would build a new life, but the community and culture they had loved would disappear for them both. Sure, they would go to the tribal celebrations when they came to the fairgrounds. Sandy saw their pain and isolation when she checked on them months later. That was enough to make Sandy think twice about staying on with the Bureau. Isolation was not her goal. She always loved the area around Bolder and applied for a police officer opening there. She had met the Bolder Sheriff back when he was called in to assist in the county where they had found Tiny Bear, and they had worked the case together.

Now both Sandy and that sheriff were in Bolder. Although he was pleased to see her when she walked into his office, he was surprised to hear she was here to pick up an application. Wasn't she an attorney? Bolder police department. Officer Sandy Curly Fox. She was more than welcome. He could more than use her insight and perspective around Bolder and the local reservation.

Sandy Curly Fox wasn't the first woman on the force, but she was the first part-Indian one. Male or female. There were tribal health offices in town and plenty of tribal members she already knew. Sandy felt like she could make a difference. Open doors. It might take a while for them to accept her, but she'd felt they would in time.

She didn't think this Lizzie needed any of her help. Sandy, however, was feeling a little more than curious that afternoon when she decided to walk back around the museum—back to where she had seen Lizzie that morning. There were still a few tracks in the snow, in front of the iron door they seemed to get mashed together a lot—almost like someone was trying to cover their tracks. Sandy knew a lot about tracks—Gramma G. had taught her a lot about them. It sure did look like someone stopped here in front of the door before they went down the hill. No one had lived in the hotel for at least fifty years, so what was she thinking? Sandy felt a cold chill run down her back. Ghosts. She grew up with lots of spirit tales. She had heard the tales of Maddie Bolder walking the riverbanks, crying for something she seemed to have lost. Sandy being Irish and Indian, was twice as superstitious as the next person. Cop or no cop, she felt something cross her path. She tried to listen to those feelings. They usually were correct. Came in real handy in her line of work.

Chapter 20

Ranger Drew Bellow

"Is this what you were talking about the other day, Sandy?" snarled Drew, totally disgusted by what he was reading.

"MAN SENTENCED TO 28 YEARS FOR SEXUALLY ABUSING TWO UNDERAGE GIRLS

Bolder (AP)—A registered sex offender will spend the next 28 years in prison for abducting, raping, and sexually abusing two underage girls. The Register-Guard reports 24-year-old Rueben Lorenzo Alvarez, of Jackson, pleaded guilty earlier this month to two counts of rape and sodomy. Additional charges of rape and strangulation were dropped as a plea agreement, as only two of the original five girls would testify."

"Yeah, a real sweetie, that one. The judge and D.A. suspected he was guilty of a bunch of other rapes but could only get him on this one. There are other instances: a missing girl who had been staying with his family, and a sister—no one seems to know where she is. The guy is a real psycho, he kept doing it even though he knew they were onto him. The registered sex offender rap was from him abusing a fourteen-year-old and another thirteen-year-old girl who was staying at their house a few years back. They were all minors at the time. They told a teacher who had him arrested. After that, both girls supposedly went back to Mexico. No one seems to know for sure. At least he's locked up now. I wish I'd had an opportunity to shoot the asshole of the universe (AOTU) first. Save us, taxpayers, a lot of goddamn money. Twenty-eight frigging years- worth," Sandy scowled. The sex offenders were the worst of them, as far as she was concerned. Everybody knew the child molesters never got better, just sicker, and more twisted in their approach. The Internet their new favorite pathway these days.

AOTU, asshole of the universe, was a favorite acronym of Sandy's.

Andrew didn't know how Sandy did it. She wouldn't share what happened at work very often. Mostly he read something in the paper; then she might nod, acknowledging she knew about it. This one must have really bothered her since her response was an actual full-blown response, followed by her biggest adjective, AOTU, for her least favorite criminals. How Sandy kept her sanity and her tongue, wasn't something he could do. Probably, also why Drew chose to be a fish and wildlife ranger. Checking fish size, permits, licenses, unpermitted fires, and busting up an underage kegger in the woods were pretty much the gamut in Drew's world. Occasionally a hunter would miss and hit a friend. Ninety-nine percent of those were accidental. This year so far, though, he had seen more than his quota of dead guys. Four drownings in the county in his waterways. All fairly young guys too. All four were not particularly a loss to anyone, according to Sandy. The fourth one was deemed a suicide and the others accidental drownings. By the time he found them they had been in the water for several months or weeks at least. Usually, they only had a couple a year. Fishing accidents, heart attacks, boats turning over when a guy was fishing alone, usually alcohol involved. In cold water, one tends to drown fast. There hadn't been any reason to suspect foul play, no visible injuries on any of them. The suicide was "supposed" since the guy was about to get pulled in for questioning on a child abuse situation. His stepson spilled the beans. He was sure he had been molesting his little sister. He had molested the boy until he got big enough to fight back. They had been to the hospital with the girl a week ago and he had threatened his stepdad with going to the police if he didn't leave them alone. The girl had died. They thought the stepdad had split, knowing he would probably be arrested. After they found his body washed up, facedown, a half-mile down from the bridge where his wallet had been discovered, the mom and kids packed up and left town. The realtor was told to sell the house and everything in it. Sandy said they burned his things in a bonfire. The neighbors could hear party music playing, sort of loud, but under the circumstances, hadn't called the police. Everyone had an alibi, and no one gave a shit.

The neighbors thought it was more than worthy of a celebration. The guy had creeped them out too and they had tired of the screaming fights they overheard too many times. Sandy and Drew were curious, but each family had their own stories to bury. They had both tangled with him and didn't like him. Now they were hearing that other people had felt the same. Sandy usually held her tongue, but not his time. She wished she could have locked him up and he would have gotten his due in prison. Pedophiles don't do well there. She felt he got off easy by drowning. If indeed he drowned. No evidence showing otherwise. "If someone killed him, they were good." Sandy had said. Drew listened, but he had other things on his mind today than criminals.

Drew Bellows had fallen hard for Sandy, the moment she pulled in the biggest trout he had ever seen around Bolder. She had gently released it back into the current, speaking a Nez Perce blessing she remembered from school about it swimming back to its family, about it being too small for her to eat. "Maybe next year," she said. Drew had made them peanut butter and jelly sandwiches, with a couple ginger ales. Her red locks had been wildly falling out from her baseball cap, torn jeans and old tennis shoes were about the sexiest thing he had ever seen. She had out-fished him, out-hunted him, and out-hiked him. She was more than he could ever wish for. Sometimes though, like now, he knew she kept secrets from him. He knew she had lived on the reservation when she was little and that by her teens, someone named Gramma Gopher had sent her away to a private school in California. He knew Sandy was grateful to the old Indian woman, but he also knew Sandy rarely went on the "res' unless on official business these days. She was maybe three-quarter Indian, but they didn't usually include her. He noticed she spoke to the trees, the animals, and the stars in the sky just the way Gramma Gopher had taught her—with respect to the spirits—but she was a tribe of one. Drew, Sandy Curly Fox, Scout (Drew's cow dog), and Toby, the kitten he had given her, he hoped reminded Sandy they were their own tribe of four. If Drew had his way the tribe would grow. He wasn't sure how kids would fit into her lifestyle. He had a super mellow gig and could see kids in his future, but Sandy would sometimes be called out in the middle of the night for backup when things were more than their small force could handle and particularly if it involved tribe members or murders. One sensitive and her specialty, the other one homicide, requiring the sheriff.

Drugs were a problem in Bolder just like everywhere. Methamphetamine mostly, tweakers who stole anything you didn't have nailed down or locked up. Drunk drivers really pissed her off, particularly when she knew them. When she pulled over an Indian for drunk driving, and of course they knew her, they would always try and talk her out of arresting them. Rules should not apply since they were her people, "Don't you know?" Man, that really got her going. They went to jail. Then the tribal police would come and get them. They would be out in a day and back at it again. Probably another reason she didn't care to go to the reservation. At least there if she saw anything, she had no jurisdiction, but it still bugged her. It really hurt when she had to arrest the young women. Sometimes they would remember her Gramma G, and Sandy would use that moment to talk about the sobriety circles. Maybe they could try, she would get the information for them and a few did sober up, went to treatment, got their kids back. She could hear Gramma Gopher thanking her from above on those occasions. Gramma Gopher had started Al-anon on the "res" and the small but powerful group still met near the smokehouse a couple times a week. She had supported the sobriety circles, even letting them meet in her barn sometimes.

Sandy put her cup of black coffee down, leaned over, and kissed Drew on his head before she headed out the door. "Thanks for the coffee and the news honey," she said, "but don't believe everything you read in the paper, it's often just a part of the story."

"Oh, yeah," she said before closing the door. "Try and keep Toby in today. I had to track him down behind the museum early this morning. Not sure if he was hunting or he has moved in with our new neighbor."

"New neighbor?"

"I don't know, but there was a woman by the museum early this morning when I was coming home, and they seemed pretty chummy."

Drew laughed at her and said, "Buzz me when you're off shift and I'll meet you at the Pub for a drink, maybe a burger, and I'll buy you one of those new root beers they got brewing. We can walk home to some moonlight. Leave the car at the precinct. You have tomorrow off, right? Maybe we can plan on going down to the caves, camp, catch a full moon, and some stars? I'll catch us some trout!"

"Sounds possible," said Sandy, "Well, except the part about the fish. I'll bring my pole." She closed the door with a giggle and a grin. Drew knew what that meant, and he loved it. He loved her and it was time he really told her what that meant to him. He hoped with all his heart she would listen this time. He wasn't about to let her get away.

Chapter 21

Wet News and a Beer

Sandy showed up a half-hour before Drew at the Pub. It was one of the few places she felt like she could grab a beer, OK, a root beer, and relax without any of her "arrestees" coming in. She had gone to school with the owner's wife and Drew had dealt with their teenage boys when they got caught drinking in the woods. He tossed out their beer, gave them a good warning, and called their parents. He had them working campground cleanup for a couple Sundays. Seemed to have worked. At least if in the future if they drank, they would never be litterbugs. They were surprised at what people left behind in the campgrounds. "Gross" was a word he heard a few times during those cleanup activities.

As for Sandy, she had suggested to a couple guys, after a horrendous Ducks/Beavers game, that maybe they had a little too much to drink and should get a friend to drive them home from the Pub. The owners appreciated Sandy and Drew looking out for them and they did the same for the young couple, making sure they had a table away from the crowds and never teasing Sandy about her choice of non-alcoholic beers. They would be drinking for sure if they had her job.

Bolder had done a remarkable job of keeping its DUIs down. Nothing was far and rides were cheap. The bars had started picking up the cab fees. They knew who had friends that would come get their buddies and made a point of calling them to come get their friend or threatening to if they were really going to pursue driving. There were always the druggies you had to keep an eye on, but Sandy was starting to wonder if they should be more seriously looking into all these drownings. Adult swim classes? Water awareness? Don't go near the water alone? These three last drownings were younger men, well under forty anyway. Typically, it was guys over sixty boating alone. Some of these fellows had alcohol and drugs in their system, but they had been in the water too long to say whether that was a real factor. No evidence of foul play. Just bodies popping up more than usual. The main difference though was none of these guys had any friends or family who was looking for them. That was odd.

Sandy sat quietly staring at her "beer", grabbing a sweet potato fry occasionally, double-dipping in the hot ranch sauce, and thinking about the drownings. Jason Howard, a local news reporter walked up and asked, "What are you thinking so hard about Sandy?" in that radio kind of voice he was known for. "Looks deep--something a guy like me might be interested in. Somebody else drown?"

"Oh! Hi Jason, sorry you sort of startled me. Yeah, I- how'd you know I was thinking about these drownings? Your 'scooby sense' kind of creeps me out sometimes. You have ESP? Seems like a weird time of year for drownings, doesn't it? Then again things happen in threes they say. That's three."

"What about the guy whose wallet they found by the bridge? Sure it was a suicide? Family left pretty darn quick I hear. That would be four."

"Jason! How did you know about the wallet? Crap, don't tell me."

Jason saved her and let her know the kid and mom had spilled the beans on that one. "He was going to jail, and he knew it. His career would be over. He was a salesman and a part-time music instructor. Mom and son had alibis. They moved back to Texas with her family. You never know huh? A salesman for school equipment, God, I don't think I can have kids," said Jason, finishing with a whistle and shaking his head in disgust.

"I like kids! Are we having kids? Jason—you kids? No way!" Drew walked into the conversation at an odd time. He hadn't heard the other part of the conversation.

Good grief no! Sandy looked down at her belly flat as usual. Thank god. It really hadn't been on her agenda. The look on her face reminded Drew that he would have to face that fact someday or move on.

"Howdy, Drew. Sandy and I were just talking about the drownings. What's your call, Drew? You were the one that found them. First officer at the scene, right?" asked Jason.

"I think they are just stupid loaded guys on the water, Jason. Happens. At least we are down on kids drowning. The free classes at the pool are really having an impact. It's been a few years since we have lost any kids, so this is just a normal count if you're counting. Just all around the same time, same age…does make you wonder."

"I'm counting," said Jason. "The reporter in me says something is up. These guys were all jerks from what I understand. Maybe somebody is doing us all a favor and killing child molesters. Wouldn't that be something! A serial vigilante of perverts and pedophiles!"

Jason had to write some of the police reports, and he knew, better than most, there were too many creeps on the streets playing the catch and release game. Sandy was going to ask Jason about his sources. He might be right, these guys all seem to have poor reputations. What if he was right and she had a serial killer here in Bolder?

Just then Andrea, the bartender, passed by to see if they needed new drinks and maybe a burger. "On the house, guys, not you Jason. I'm still holding last week's tab for you."

"Oh, and I'm sorry I overheard what you guys were talking about. From what I know we should have at least five more of those creeps drowning," sniped Andrea.

"Are you talking about those five exes of yours fondly again?" snickered Jason.

"Yep, and maybe that guy who just picked up his last check too," she spat.

"Who's that?" asked Sandy

"Rueben's brother, Alphonso, the guy in the paper yesterday. Rueben's getting 28 years at least. His brother is just as guilty. I've seen the work he has done to his so-called girlfriends. They call themselves Fang Gang, bloodsuckers, and I wouldn't be surprised if that implies, they suck the life out of young girls. I've seen them go over to the motel with girls that don't look more than fourteen. The guys in the kitchen, they talk. They don't realize I understand a fair amount of Spanish myself. They joke that Alphonso has a really, big family, lots of little sisters. Mucho Grande Familia."

"Why haven't you said something, Andrea?" asked Sandy.

"Not like we have a chance for long chats officer," she replied. "Want that root beer?"

"Dos Cervesas por favor mi amigos."

"Two of your famous root beers please; hold the burgers and a Pale ale for Jason please," said Drew. "I'll buy his."

Andrea's comments were interesting, thought all three of them. Mainly because all three had been wondering about these guys themselves. There had been a new element around town this last summer. Usually leaves when the growing season is over, but from what Andrea was saying maybe there was a new crop in town. Walking on two legs.

Sex trafficking wasn't a new thing to Sandy, she had heard about it and worked a case back in Colorado. But here in Bolder? Ag town, USA. Cowboys and Indians. Sex trafficking? That's city stuff, right? Seattle, Portland, San Francisco…

Just then three gals and a big guy sat down at the bar where Jason had just come from. They ordered three Storm Warning Winter Ales, a specialty here at the Pub. Rich, hearty brew for sure. Must be getting cold.

"I'll have an iced tea with lemon please," asked the brunette with the flowered Dansko clogs. The others had on regular nursing Crocs, green. Hospital staff thought Sandy. Then she realized the brunette was the woman that had been with her cat, Toby, the other morning. She thought she'd excuse herself to the ladies' room momentarily, walk by and check her out. Maybe say hello?

"Hi, remember me?" asked Sandy, "The other day behind the museum?"

"Oh, yeah, Toby's Mom! How is he doing? Staying home in this weather I hope?"

"Seems to have come to his senses. Thanks for looking out for him."

"I'm guessing from those snazzy shoes and mean greenies you all are wearing you all work at the hospital?" asked Sandy.

"Yeah," said the big guy, we are all in the E.R. Long night, last night."

Sandy took this as an opportunity. "Hey any of you know- I mean strictly off the record. I know you have the HIPA rights and all that, but are you seeing any of the signs associated with sex trafficking? Young girls with injuries and no identification? Don't speak English? That kind of thing? Brought in by a 'friend of the family?'"

"Just the run of the mill wife beatings last night, but we sure are glad to see that Rueben character get the time. Fairly sure we took care of his messes a few too many times. Makes you sick. It's ugly. But you know that. Yeah, I know who you are," the big guy said.

"Sheriff Fox, nice to see you somewhere else other than the door of our ER."

Andrea brought the drinks to the hospital crew just as Alphonso went out the door. "Last check for that scumbag. Guess he's leaving town too. Sorry, it's not in the police van with his brother."

The brunette didn't say a thing but watched him leave, which made Sandy think she knew something. Not a peep. Only thing standing out about her were her shoes and maybe how little she really was. Couldn't be more than a hundred pounds. She had only seen her that day with a sweatshirt on and boots. Petite gal, quiet too.

Sandy watched her, as Lizzie observed Alphonso walk out the double doors to the parking lot.

A few minutes later, Lizzie excused herself and slipped off towards the restrooms.

"You all from Bolder?" asked Sandy.

"Am now," said two of them. "Lizzie and I are on contract," said the big nurse. "I think she is from Oakland or something. I'm from Wyoming. Maybe this town's too big for me now with you guys talking about sex trafficking. Only traffic we got is an elk stampede where I come from!"

They all laughed and ordered another round. Sandy went back to her table. Drew whispered in Sandy's ear, "Remember I asked if you wanted to go camping tomorrow? We better get going if we want to hit the road early."

As they walked out, Sandy noticed Lizzie standing by the bus stop. Looking small and alone, probably not a good idea in this neighborhood at night. No buses coming soon that she knew of on this route after five.

"Need a ride?" asked Sandy.

"No thanks, I'm just waiting for a friend. I'm sure they will be here anytime now."

Across the parking lot, Sandy noticed Alphonso packing up an old blue low rider Mercury Grand Marquis with bench seating. You don't see many of those anymore. Maybe in Los Angeles, but not in snow country. Looks like he had been staying at the motel next door to the Pub. Kind of expensive for a kitchen worker.

He was alone. Seemed to be in a bit of a hurry. Back seat was full of used liquor boxes, overstuffed green garbage bags, and what looked like a pink My Little Pony backpack in the passenger seat. Things were just tossed in there helter-skelter like he was getting out of town fast. Wherever he was going it didn't look like he was taking anyone with him. Not that she could see anyway. The way the guy looked; she wouldn't be surprised if there was a body in the trunk. She didn't have any probable cause. Just a good imagination it seemed.

She turned around and Lizzie had disappeared. That girl, she swore, was a spook!

Maybe she really did need a night under the stars with Drew. She was getting to look at everybody like they might be up to something. Not everybody is up to no good, Sandy thought to herself. You need a few days off!

Chapter 22

Back in the E.R.

Lizzie stood at the bus stop just long enough for someone to see her standing there. It had been Officer Fox who asked if she needed a ride someplace. Hopefully, she wouldn't have noticed her jeans and blue tennis shoes. Lizzie was quite the quick-change artist. She'd gone in the bathroom to change out of her scrubs before she left the Pub. It had occurred to her if she were to have made friends here in Bolder that Officer Fox and her man, Drew, could have been fun, interesting, and possibly a great source of local criminal activity! She could do without the snoopy reporter. Somebody who might have watched national or international news might recognize her. Although she had been extremely secretive about herself, it was not always possible to stay out of the public eye around her parents. Good grief thought Lizzie, police, and reporters were the last people she should be making friends with these days. Four down, one to go.

Sandy and Drew reminded her of folks Lizzie had worked with inside the Christian medical missions or with Doctors Without Borders. They genuinely cared about what they did, had a good camaraderie about the county and its issues, but still took time to enjoy the beautiful area they worked in. She wondered what it would be like to go out in the country with them, particularly exploring Captain Jack's Stronghold. She had overheard Drew talking to the reporter about the last Indian war with the Modocs and if she guessed right, Sandy had first-hand knowledge of the local reservation. Lizzie saw the Indian features in her. These two had stories to tell and those were the kind of folks she really enjoyed. When she traveled with her father and mother through California, Mexico, and then having lived in Brazil, it was hearing the local lore that made the journey so colorful. You always learned more through visiting with the old-timers than through any books or magazines—just like tonight. She missed exploring the cultures around where she worked. Maybe she would volunteer down in Mexico on its southern borders. Thousands were fleeing Central America and they had medical and mobile clinics set up along the route. It was time to move on, too many bodies for this time of year, according to what she overheard Jason, the reporter say.

Last night, she heard just that "little bit more" that she had needed to know about Alphonso. She saw his car and now knew where he was staying. Perfect timing. More importantly, that he was leaving, and obviously soon.

Two nights ago, Alphonso had been in the E.R. with a woman and a teenage girl. When they brought her in, she wouldn't talk to anyone and the woman checking her in said she was visiting from El Salvador and had been in a car accident. After her examination, it was noted that she had a broken arm and nose and multiple bruises on her arms and inside her thighs. All typical signs of abuse and, probably, sexual abuse.

"Did someone do this to you?" Lizzie asked, holding her hands gently, using her almost perfect Spanish to the delight of the E.R. doctor that night who didn't know a lick of it. The girl's eyes were puffy, red from crying and cheap black mascara was running down her face. She wouldn't look up.

"Si," she whispered, still not looking up.

"Where did they hurt you?" Lizzie asked gently.

She started crying, her big, beautiful brown eyes now looking up at Lizzie. A look that sealed somebody's fate.

"We can help you find a safe place, but you need to tell us what happened, who did this?" said Lizzie.

Lizzie could see the girl, stiffen, then, her head in her hands, said, "The man told the woman to go fix me up, that I was no good to him now and to hurry. They were leaving in the morning. They are going to sell me to another man tomorrow, in another town not far from here, or as soon as I can work again. Please don't make me go. I would rather die." Her brown eyes pleaded with Lizzie.

The tall, heavyset male nurse went out to the waiting room and told the woman the girl would need to stay the night. Could they stay and fill out some paperwork at the desk, please? The woman fidgeted, obviously nervous, the man grabbed her arm and said, "Okay, we will be right back." Of course, they never saw them again.

Ok, not entirely true. Lizzie saw him picking up his final check at the Creamery. She knew there was sex trafficking going on in Bolder. But talking about it wasn't going to change anything. Seriously, his brother might be getting twenty-eight to thirty years on your tax dollars, but Alphonso only had a few more hours if Lizzie had anything to do with it. Lizzie was feeling lucky and ready for just one more. Her contract was up in a few days and from what Jason and Sandy were saying, they were getting to be too many bodies popping up around Bolder these days.

Chapter 23

Need a Ride?

"Hey, Chica, need a ride? It's kind of dark. What are you doing here alone?" Alphonso was fishing of course, but you never know, he might get lucky. "Nice flowers," he says.

"Yes, for my sister, it's her birthday." Responds Lizzie, holding the flowers wrapped in plastic by her side.

The long auburn braid going down her back, her jeans, blue tennis shoes, and her small frame made her look just like the young girls this guy went after. Lizzie stepped over to the car and said, "Really? thanks, I missed the bus, and they don't come again tonight."

Alphonso thought, she is going to be late, like never arrive... she looks about twelve, maybe thirteen. I'll have a little fun with her myself and then she can easily replace that whore I left at the hospital. Perfecto!

Lizzie kept her head down as she got in the car, her hat shielding her face from any scrutiny. He tosses the "my little pony" backpack over the bench seat. Lizzie wonders who that had belonged to. She told him where she needed to go, towards the side of town where the river and canyon are located. He took off slowly turning towards the industrial area, not where she had asked him to go. Things are going differently than planned. She had hoped he would head towards the park at least. She asks nervously where he is going, and he says he has one stop first before he can drop her off. He drives toward a commercial-industrial area not far from the Pub. It's after hours in this part of town. No one to hear you scream. That's what Alphonso thinks anyway. It has worked for him in the past.

She is more than ready. A good dose of Devil's Breath in the needle she just slipped out of the flowers. He parks, turns towards her, leans into her, and holds her left hand. She takes her right hand and stabs him in the neck with the syringe. Startled he goes to grab her other arm, but it's too late for Alphonso. The devil is already numbing his mind and Lizzie is moving away. Lizzie steps out of the car. In a few minutes, he might be dead or at least not moving.

"What the fu…?" He is having trouble breathing, he can't speak. He falls over on the seat, his face bulging, spittle coming from his mouth, his eyes wide open. She closes them for him.

Lizzie opens his door and pushes him over to the passenger side, puts the lap belt on. Props him up so he looks asleep. These old cars with the bench seats make it a lot easier, she thinks. He just looks like he's passed out. It is late after all.

Good thing he is a short and scrawny guy. She barely reaches the pedals, then finds the seat control and moves it up an inch. Thanking the gods that the car is an automatic, she gets in and drives towards the canyon. The first part of this didn't work out the way she planned but the end would be the same. Just don't get stopped she hoped…

About a mile out of town the river meanders below in a steep canyon. Nice dirt road, great place for kids to park, do drugs and make out; school night, no one there this night. Just Lizzie and Alphonso. He won't be giving rides to anyone ever again.

She pulls up close to the edge, puts it in park, unbuckles Alphonso and pushes him back towards the driver's seat, a branch and rock under the wheel for just a minute— then she puts it back in drive, removes the rock, and the branch. It creeps forward slowly and then crashes over the edge flipping upside down into the river three hundred feet below, floating briefly in the current. "Adios, Alphonso!"

Just a half a mile walk back to the museum to say goodbye—lock it up tight. Then to the apartment where she would take a shower, pick up her few belongings in the studio, leaving a note for the cocktail waitress, who had a place across the hall, to keep anything she left behind and a note for the housekeeper to toss or donate the rest. She left her a little cash too. Lizzie didn't need anything. She was leaving Bolder. Grateful for the half-moon, quiet school nights, and the train station within walking distance. She was leaving Bolder a better place.

That night had been her last night in town. Amtrak came thru in the morning at 7:30, and she would be on it. J.J. and her lovely Belle of Oakland would hook up again soon, but not right now. She needed time to process. Was she getting reckless?

"Maybe Eugene? Portland? Seattle this time? "Lizzie said out loud to Lilly. "I hear they have quite a problem in Eugene and Portland. Lilly? What say you?"

"Go Home," Lizzie imagined she heard Lilly say. Or was that another voice in her head?

She felt the presence of Bao.

He was standing at the end of the bottom of the stairs. A's baseball cap over a concerned, albeit curious expression. It was his voice in a tone she had only heard once before, commanding, and clear. "Come on down, Lizzie. It's time we go home. I think we may have some catching up to do."

Chapter 24

Enter Bao

The night before, Bao had gotten a room at the motel near the Pub, thinking he would surprise Lizzie tomorrow morning on her way to Amtrak. He knew she was planning on leaving Bolder tomorrow by train. Why not surprise her with J.J. and the La Belle for a ride home?

He was checking into his room when he saw her step into an old blue Mercury Marquis with a little Mexican guy at the wheel. She looked like she knew what she was doing, but Bao's intuition was screaming that something wasn't right in Kansas, as Dorothy liked to say in the Wizard of Oz. A favorite of Lizzie's.

Quickly he went to his rental car and followed them, sure to stay just far enough behind. The Mexican went around the corner and parked. Bao turned off his lights and parked a building away. Just a few minutes later, Lizzie got out and got in the driver's side. Something was off here.

He knew how much Lizzie hated driving. The driver was now leaning over as if he had passed out. Was Lizzie into drugs? Ridiculous. If anybody knew what drugs did to people, Lizzie had seen her fill in Sao Paulo, years ago. She surely saw enough overdoses in ER.

Whatever was going on, she was now pulling away. He followed her a few miles, keeping a good distance. Not hard here in Bolder at this time of night. He pulled over into a neighborhood market as he saw her go down a dirt road. He sat for about five minutes, parked, lights off, just wondering what she was up to, thinking maybe he should follow her. About five minutes later she walked out of the bushes near the dirt road she had driven down, squeezing through a barbed wire fence, and jumping the gully. She looked around, towards the market, and then walked down the hill towards town.

153

She seemed fine. With just enough moonlight he could see that Lizzie was smiling that little smile of hers just like after she'd been flying her crazy loop de loops. Whatever had happened with her and that blue sedan seemed to have made her happy. Bao didn't have a clue what or if he would say anything to Lizzie about this. She would be furious that he had followed her. He knew she didn't live far from here and could get herself home. Lizzie was always aware of her surroundings and quite capable of handling herself. She had lived in much more dangerous places than Bolder and survived. He would just return to the hotel and go see her first thing in the morning. She had some talking to do and something told him it wasn't going to be easy.

Something still bugged him. Where did the guy and the car go? Was there a house back there she had taken him to? His worry got the best of him as usual when it came to Lizzie, so he got out of the rental car and walked down the dirt road. With the moon and his iPhone flashlight, he could see well enough. Not far off the main road was a canyon with a river below. The road dead-ended at the cliff. He looked over the edge, but it was too dark to see the river now. Clouds were obscuring the moon now. No blue sedan here. Nothing, but fresh tire tracks going off the edge. Just the sound of the river flowing below, some mist in the canyon, and the cool breeze coming up the granite canyon walls from the frigid waters below.

He needed to talk to her about this, maybe. But right now, it would wait. Tomorrow they would do some catching up. He decided not to say anything unless she brought it up. We all had secrets. He'd stay with his plan, he needed to bring her home. Oddly enough when he met her that next morning, she agreed. Even before he told her about Cookie and why he was here.

She didn't seem surprised to see him. Not at all. He usually called first. So, when Bao appeared like this it wasn't good. Someone was missing, someone had died, something was wrong. What would make him come to her without warning, face to face? Did he know about her little outings? How long had he been here in Bolder?

Chapter 25

Sandy and Drew Make Two

Sandy and Drew enjoyed the night sky down at The Stronghold. Awesome thing about being the girlfriend of a ranger was that he knew just the spots in the park they could be alone in, under the stars, away from any prying eyes. Early spring camping was always brisk; you never knew if the last snow had fallen or not, but it was also the only time they could have a fire these days. She loved a crackling fire. It reminded her of the good times when she was a little red-headed Indian girl, and nobody chastised her for her red locks. Little kids don't care. Wish we could keep that wonder and non-judgmental thinking that is lost with growing up. She was just thankful for the gifts Gramma Gopher had given her. This night, she knew Drew had something he wanted to talk to her about. He had been unusually quiet last night, going straight to bed after gathering up everything for the camp trip. They were only going for a weekend, but you would think they were setting up house from the looks of everything in the truck. Just enough space left for Drew, his dog, Scout, and Sandy. It had been a year since they had met, basically the same as they had been dating. He and Scout stayed in the carriage house at the House of Seven Gables, more than not. When he wasn't there, she missed him. Was that a sign? Even Toby liked the dog. Was this going to lead to marriage? Not like she had any role models for marriage. She never really considered it much, one way or another. It never really seemed to go with her career choices.

There was that realtor, an adorable little old gal, Betty, that she had worked with, who had been married for like sixty years and to the same person, a true rarity these days! She really missed her husband, who had recently passed and often would share such wonderful stories of their life together. Their family, friends, and travels while he was in the military.

Sandy had bought the purple seven gables house from her the day she took the job. They had gotten to be good buddies and Betty teased Drew. "When was he going to make an honest woman of Sandy?" More like an honest man of Drew. He was the old-fashioned one of the two. Betty's husband and Gramma Gopher had passed over about the same time, so not only buying the cool old, haunted house but grieving together had really bonded them. Betty was surprised when Sandy moved into the adjacent carriage house and rented out the main house. Sandy loved the big old house and planned on doing some remodeling one of these days before moving into it. In the beginning, she was comfortable in the carriage house. The view of the river canyon from the upstairs of the sweet cottage was amazing, anyway. It had a one-butt kitchen. Perfect for Sandy, who never cooked anyway. Drew loved to cook, and honestly, he did better than she did. However, she out-fished him, as she so often loved to remind him. They had stopped in the lower canyon, where of course Sandy caught a sixteen-inch rainbow trout, and of course, Drew got skunked. She brought the lemons. He brought the root beer. Drew knew he would lose the bet they had made last night on who would be the first to catch some trout. She always won. He purchased the root beer earlier in the week. He didn't care, he had something bigger on his line he wanted to reel in.

It had been a fantastic and magical day. Big blue skies, surrounded by mountains, triumphant river time, some spelunking in the caves, showing Sandy the deep fern cave—her first magical time down there. He thought he knew everything about the last Indian war, the Modoc War. Sandy had her own version that she grew up with and it gave him another view of this woman he loved. That night she told him stories of the mountains and how "the people" came to be here. Although he had a tad of Indian blood in him, it was so far removed he figured it was just fodder for the mill of stories where his family came from. There was no record of Drew's ancestry, just talk; he would have to do one of those Ancestry.com things one day. He really liked that she had a history, that she kept the good stuff and had learned to leave the bad behind. Like just drinking root beer. Instead of alcohol. We all have a story, he thought. He wasn't going to wait any longer to find out if she would be in his. He had her cousin, an amazing Indian artist, and jeweler, make a gold band of feathers with a small diamond, like a star, on one end of the feathers that he thought he would give to her first of the year. He didn't want to wait any longer. No doubts in his mind. He wanted Sandy Curly Fox, kids, or no kids. He had accepted that she hadn't spoken about them being in her future. But she had talked about opening a center for kids to hang out at after school and even a safe house for the ones who can't go home. If that's how they had kids, that would work too. They both had seen enough homeless teens these days.

Sandy told a few of Gramma G's old Indian tales, then they just sat quietly by the fire, listening to the coyotes, and waiting for falling stars. Drew waited until both witnessed a shooting star brightly streaking across their path.

"Something to wish on!" he said, "I get to go first since you got the fish!"

He looked straight into her eyes. "Oh, how I wish Sandy Curly Fox would marry me and make me the happiest man on this earth." She looked at him in wonder, with love, curious if he was serious. He took her hands and kneeled in front of her, the ring in his hand. "I love you, Sandy Curly Fox. I have since the day I met you. Will you marry me?"

Sandy looked up to the night sky and asked, "Gramma G? What do you think?"

A second burst of stars going in the same direction past overhead just then. A meteor- shower? A perfect blessing direct from Gramma G. How could she say no.

"Yes, Ranger Drew, I will marry you, I can't promise we will be the happiest people on earth every day… life does take its turns sometimes, but at least we can try!" They both laughed out loud. With tears of joy in their eyes, Drew slipped the golden ring of feathers with its little sparkle on her finger and then put his arms around her. They held each other under God and all her ancestors. The moon shining and the stars twinkling to them all the happiness in the world.

The sparks of their small fire rising into the night sky sealed his wish and rose high to mingle with the spirit of Sandys Gramma Gopher. They had never felt more blessed.

Chapter 26

Three Months Later

Sandy, Drew, Scout, and Toby got married on the front porch of the purple House of Seven Gables. The tenants had given notice the day after the proposal and they both thought it was a good sign that it was time to move into the big house and stretch out. Drew had an amazing amount of stuff, Sandy came to find out. That was OK. since she didn't have much in the carriage house anyway and she'd finally get the Indian baskets, beads, and pottery she'd had in storage at Gramma G's all these years out and display them properly. They moved in a couple of months after the starry proposal and a quick remodel. Drew had a huge kitchen now with a wolf range and a chopping block island with all his favorite pots on display. In the evenings, Scout and Toby shared the window seat facing the back of the museum. Like they were looking for something. Why didn't they take the one looking at the river? A better view, more wildlife. Sandy wondered, once, if Toby was waiting for Lizzie to come back. Cats are funny like that, not always entirely loyal like dogs. They never saw her again after the night at the Creamery. Sandy had seen her at the bus stop briefly. Lizzie had blue tennis shoes, jeans, and her hair in a long braid. She didn't have her scrubs or those spendy flowered Dansko nurse shoes on. Cops remember weird stuff. Drew always reminded her that she had a brain that nothing could sneak by, but she couldn't help but wonder about that woman. Drew's "Scooby" sense felt it too. They'd seen the hospital crew again a week later and asked about her—the pretty little brunette?

"Lizzie?" They all chimed in at the same time.

"The short girl with the flowered crocs?" asked Sandy

"Yeah, that's her," said big nurse guy. "Basic scrubs like the rest of us, but always expensive shoes, Danskos. Well, she was Locum Tenens, but a traveler, all the same, they're different. She left immediately when her contract was up. I heard, like the next day. Never really got to know her. She kept to herself mostly. It's okay, we expect that with them. They get ants in their pants and have to move on."

"Problems?" asked Sandy

"Nope, she was very professional. We loved that she spoke Spanish fluently and didn't get into the docs like most of the travelers do, looking for a quick romance. No, Lizzie was different. Nice, quiet, but different. Would have liked to see her stick around if you know what I mean. Big guy like me probably wouldn't have had a chance with her anyway."

"Hey Sammy, don't be so hard on yourself. That girl had other things going on. We all knew it. Came from money, that one. She wasn't in it for the dough. Didn't flirt with the docs like some guys or gals," snickered green-shoes nurse. "How about you look over here?" she said teasingly to Big Guy.

Just then, saved by the bell, as they say, Sandy's phone vibrated, as did Drew's. They both saw the text at the same time. Drew picked up the check, paid it quickly and they both headed out the door.

Chapter 27

Presents of Many Kinds

"Looks like he has been there at least three months," remarked the diver.

"I'm no forensic specialist, but I am kind of curious how he got here. No bridges close by that he would have driven off. The car is packed with stuff—he was going somewhere," said the diver.

"Don't think he got there!" said one of the guys who had found the car washed up on the shore with the body still strapped in it. It was gross with the fish and crawdads still nibbling on him and crawling out of his pants.

"Guessing it's not a suicide, nor a drowning—maybe he just ticked somebody off? Drug deal gone bad at the last minute. Was he shot? Stabbed?" asked Sandy.

"No bullet holes I can see," said the diver. "The pathologist will have to look him over good though, he's pretty messed up."

"Still, he looks familiar," said Sandy.

"How can you tell?" asked Drew. "I mean …"

"The car, the whole picture Drew, I feel like I've seen this before." Then she noticed the My Little Pony backpack in the back seat. Alphonso. It had to be. "Alphonso," she said out loud.

Sandy looked at her deputy. "Check it out, see if he has any prints left, any ID, call the pub and see if he left a forwarding address. I'm sure it's him. Foul play would not be a surprise if it's who I think it is."

"Hard to believe, but I missed breakfast and lunch today with all this going on. I'm starving," said Sandy. "You want to go grab a bite? Maybe we should go down to the pub ourselves, anyway, and ask some questions?"

Amazing how this woman could think of food after looking at this dead guy for hours, thought Drew. That's my gal.

"I could swear you looked like you had something else on your mind anyway, Drew, want to share?"

"Actually, I do have something interesting to show you," said Drew.

"And we have got another dead guy in the river…I want to get the whole picture before we leave here, then I want to hear all about it, Drew."

A half-hour later, the car was completely pulled out of the river, and the body was on the way to the morgue. Sandy and Drew were on their way to the Pub.

They ordered a couple burgers smothered with cheese and mushrooms with sweet potato fries. Two icy root beers. Drew put an envelope on the table in front of Sandy.

"Kind of odd, but the curator, Niles, from the Bolder Museum called and said he had an official-looking letter for us. It was mailed to the museum. Our names were on it. He remembered us from all the times we had met while looking for Toby around the museum. He found it unusual, figured whoever sent the letter just had the wrong address. It's from a law firm in Oakland, California. Anyway, you open it. Maybe someone left us their fortune!"

"More likely a lawsuit from someone I arrested or a court subpoena," whined Sandy.

Sandy opened the envelope and held a letter from an attorney in Oakland and a notecard.

Written on the notecard in small cursive type was this:

Mrs. Sandy Curly Fox and Mr. Drew Bellows,

Congratulations on your recent marriage. I wish you the most happiness and I know you will make good use of this at your new youth center. With great hopes for your future success. All the best.

No signature. Nada.

They held a letter that asked them to contact the local attorney assigned to this gift, for wire instructions, so they could wire a donation to the Scouts & Stars Youth Center. Sandy and Drew had started the center with small donations and lots of personal labors. Many friends and the tribal council even pitched in. The local teens had also got involved, helping them with design and details of what the kids really could use. They would be able to meet so many needs with this incredible donation. The wire was for five million dollars! The letter from an attorney in Oakland-Benson & Howell, Law Offices. Kate Benson, attorney, wished them the best and reminded them this was a private and anonymous donation. It was their fiduciary duty to not ever disclose their client's name. She looked forward to hearing how the progress was going at the center sometime. Her email and office number were all on the letterhead. Should they send a thank you note? Call? Who would they call?

Drew and Sandy looked at each other, the letter sitting on the table between them now. They had no idea where it came from. Neither of them knew anybody with that kind of money. Not around Bolder, that was for sure. They had hit everybody up in town and it was getting dry. There were lots of needs in a small village like theirs and lots of hands out. And now there seemed to be more young homeless people on the move. This was going to really help so many. They couldn't believe what had just fallen out of the sky, as far as both were concerned.

"What do we do?" asked Sandy with tears in her eyes knowing what great good this could do.

"Just like it says, put it to good use" Drew said with a smile. "I have to be honest, I wished for more than you when I wished on those stars the night of my proposal, Sandy. I knew we might never have children of our own, but this will let us help a lot of other kids."

"About that," said Sandy with a big grin. She patted her barely visible tummy.

"No way!" Drew stared at her in disbelief, but total joy.

"Yep, two months along," Sandy said right before she inhaled the rest of her burger.

He couldn't believe it. He had told her he would love to have kids, but it was OK if they didn't. He had made peace that she never talked about having kids. He knew it had been a tough childhood for her. Even with Gramma G's loyalty and love.

"I like the name Elizabeth if it's a girl," announced Sandy between big bites.

"Hmmm…" Still in shock of just finding out he'd be a dad in 7 months. "Where did you come up with that? Family name?" asked Drew.

"Not a clue darling Drew, not a clue. OK, maybe something I had in a dream the other night…"

"What if it's a boy?"

"Doubtful. Gramma G was in the dream and she was holding a little brown-haired baby girl. She was quite lovely with big amber eyes."

Drew knew Sandy well enough not to question her "dreams," particularly those with Gramma G in them. Today was the best day of his life, he chose to just go with that,

"Elizabeth it is."

Chapter 28

Home

Lizzie, Bao, and JJ had traveled on the Pullman back towards Oakland to the Lakehouse. They stopped briefly to look at Castle Crags and take a look at the Sacramento River flowing south towards the valley. It was all so beautiful and quiet. Just the sound of the train grumbling while it uncoupled some cars in Dunsmuir. They would be back home tonight. Bao had plenty of things to talk about on the way home. First would be how they would take care of Cookie who had recently been diagnosed with colon cancer. Her amazing energy force was fading fast, and Bao knew Lizzie would want to come home and take care of Cookie herself. He wanted to be the one to tell Lizzie about Cookie directly. He gave her the full update over coffee that morning on the train. Family updates always came first. She knew something was up or he would never have just arrived at her doorstep unannounced. Bao didn't do that kind of thing. Lizzie could also feel something different between them. It wasn't just the tension and worry about Cookie either. He would tell her eventually. They never kept secrets from each other. OK, she had five secrets right now. For his own good, she would keep those to herself.

How amazingly breathtaking the area of Northern California and Southern Oregon were as they rolled by chugging along on the train. Thick pine forests, lakes, and then undulating golden hills with ancient oak tree stands standing guard on top of them. Bao could understand why she had decided to stay up there for a while. He would never have arrived like he did if it hadn't been that Cookie had so suddenly taken ill. And the truth was he was getting a little curious about what Lizzie's life was like out there in her world. John and Sarah had made Bao promise to look out for her if anything ever happened to them.

John wasn't sure a day would come that Lizzie would come into the company. She couldn't be a gypsy- nurse, forever, right? Surely, she would meet someone and have a family of her own someday? Bao wasn't sure at all what Lizzie was up to, but he had been ready to find out, one way or another. He had googled the local newspaper in Bolder, out of curiosity, more than anything, what was the draw there for her. Lots of small-town news. Obituaries, crime, new businesses opening, upcoming elections. Something caught his interest, however. An unusual number of drownings, particularly of young men, for a small community like Bolder, a reporter had written. Three younger men just in the last 6 months. Drownings. True, young men didn't usually drown unless alcohol or drugs were involved. He wondered if Lizzie had heard about them. They would have gone straight to the morgue not, to ER. She might have been interested if she had read the local newspaper. He wasn't sure if she even read papers anymore. Neither of them had forgotten about what Gregor looked like that day or Lilly floating out there, he was sure. They never talked about it— maybe this would be a good way to see how she was doing these days. Had she read the local news? What did she think about the drownings? How did Lizzie deal with her demons? Bao just worked non-stop. The company was his life. He had dated occasionally, mostly friends set him up, but no one had ever really interested him. Even if someone did, what kind of life would that be for a wife. He traveled incessantly. He was looking forward to taking some time off, helping with Cookie until the end as much as she would let him. He had hired a Cambodian-speaking nurse to assist her in bathing and dressing. Cookie would allow that. The doctor said it wouldn't be long now. He also felt a real need to spend time with Lizzie. Who was she now and what did she want to do with the rest of her life? And who was in that car? What did she have to do with that? After they were settled in at the cabin, he would find the right time to talk.

Lizzie decided to stay in the main house, though, to be closer to Cookie if she needed her in the night. She would accept Lizzie's loving care and nursing skills, after all, she had delivered Lizzie! Bao was happy Lizzie made that decision on her own. He wasn't entirely comfortable being too close to her in the cabin this trip, even though he was hoping for some alone time with her. Something was different about Lizzie and until he knew what it was, he felt a view from a distance would be best. She still looked like his Lizzie, young and beautiful, but a subtle and dangerous energy was emanating from her now. More than that, he was good at telling when someone had some other agenda. She seemed strangely empowered. And oddly happier than he had remembered seeing her in years.

Chapter 29

Next

The weeks flew by with Cookie disappearing before their very eyes. Her spirit was strong, but her body kept shrinking. Cookie would not let Lizzie give her much of the morphine the doctors had prescribed, preferring to use her own herbal tinctures from her kettle of Cambodian potions. Cookie preferred the traditional Cambodian cupping and coining, to deal with her ills. Lizzie, of course, found this quite intriguing, and Cookie enjoyed passing on to Lizzie the old ways she had brought from the jungle, so many years ago. Indeed, she had used some of these same potions and applications with Sarah when she was giving birth to the twins in the jungle so many years ago. Cookie knew better than most what she needed and what would work for her. She wanted to be aware of what was going on around her, to be a part of it all until the spirits took her. Western medicine took the spirit away, as well as the pain, she thought. She would prefer to keep some pain. She wanted to see it all until she saw her angels who went before her. She held her old coin, having Lizzie lubricate it and rub her shoulders and neck until she fell deep asleep. Lizzie didn't understand it, but it seemed to relax the ancient wonder she had known all her life. She had learned so much from Cookie. If Cookie only knew.

Cookie was honored that her secrets would not die with her and she hoped that Lizzie would find good use somehow for the old ways she taught her. Sarah always adhered to them, although she had never told John. They had been secret scientists here in the arboretum, right under John's nose. Lizzie had been curious from a young age on how the plants worked in the medicinal sense, particularly the lethal plants. As Cookie remembered this, she wondered about Lizzie. She knew Bao was concerned about her, but he hadn't shared anything in depth with Cookie. Usually, he would, but not now. He was protecting her. From what she wondered. Had Cookie not had the best life ever with the Harman's? Losing Lilly was a tragedy, but Lizzie seemed to have built a life anyway, right? Cookie knew in her heart the answer to that. No, Lizzie had not built a normal life. She had never brought a man home, had never had a boyfriend, never brought friends home from school. Her only mention over the years of a true friend was that woman in Tanzania who worked with the albinos. Kathryn? She never stayed in one place long enough for roots to grow. She had been running all these years. From ghosts?

Lately, though Lizzie seemed more settled. Happy to be home, even though Cookie knew Lizzie loved her and they would be letting go of each other soon. Lizzie was a nurse, a scientist. She could smell death as well as this old witch doctor could. It would be soon. Cookie looked forward to seeing her family again, that had gone so long ago to their heavenly father. She just hoped that Lizzie would be alright and could go on too. Bao would take care of everything, like always. She hoped he could anyway.

Bao and Lizzie had been spending quite a bit of time together. He wanted her to get up to date with the family business. She had been gone for half a year and they did need her input occasionally, he would remind her. Reality was, he wanted her input. She was the biggest stockholder in the companies and eventually would need to face up to that. She could not be anonymous forever, could she? The world knew she existed, even if she preferred, they didn't. He needed her to be more present in all their lives. How he was going to do that, he wasn't quite sure yet. In the meantime, they were spending more and more time together taking care of business updates, enjoying meals on the deck by the lake, kayaking the lake, and flying around Northern California together. She even flew him down to San Diego for a meeting. Lizzie and Chuck had reconnected too. Chuck taking her out to make sure she was current in her aircrafts. They had been sitting in the hanger for six months in Oakland. He made sure they were flight-ready and Lizzie too. It was like getting on a bicycle for her. She took back to the air like a bird.

Bao, Chuck, and she flew down to Monterey for lunch one afternoon, in Chucks Mitsubishi MU-2. Lizzie had never ridden in it and wondered about the shift from the Skymaster. Chuck usually went for short take-off over occupancy, even in California. It was comfortable and could handle a good working space for eight passengers easily. Were they bringing someone back with them today? Over a long bayfront seafood feast at the Chart House by the bay, Lizzie asked Chuck what he had been up to and he openly answered her. She was spellbound at his response. After what had happened in Sao Paulo years ago, she had understood that Chuck had been involved in some clandestine activities. She had never inquired much; she knew whatever he was involved in, it was for the good of something or someone. If he had wanted to tell her, he would have. He would joke if he told her he would have to kill her. She now, truly, understood the meaning of that kind of storyline these days.

Bao quietly watched Lizzie's expression when Chuck shared a story with Lizzie about how his team and he were involved in the capture of sex traffickers in the state of Georgia recently. Over a year of investigation and undercover work, they had "assisted in" the arrest of eight adults and rescued thirty- seven kids, all crammed in an abandoned warehouse. A few were kids over sixteen that had agreed to farm work—but were really being used as sex slaves. Most were being shipped out to different areas to be used in the underground pedophile network. Sold to the highest bidder online. Lizzie told them she had treated girls she was sure were used for trafficking when she worked at Highland and even in Bolder, last year. She had helped get a couple of the girls over to Julia's safe house in Oakland when she was at Highland and then to the boarding school after they were treated and released with DHS or immigration. She had seen enough at all the hospitals she worked to know it was more of a problem, even in small towns, than people realized.

"How do you assist?" she asked, more than curious.

"We send in undercover people first— we had a nurse like you being a mole; she worked for a hospital first and then we set it up that the traffickers would call her to take care of the kids outside the hospital.

She had 'gambling' debts she couldn't cover according to them, so she worked for them. A horrible thing, but the only way we could find out who was behind this dangerous ring. This bust led to a trafficking gang around the country. Hundreds of kids were rescued. Eighteen individual procurers arrested. We slowed them down. There are lots more out there. Our undercover nurse lost her cover and is now in the witness protection plan. She'll be able to go back to work with her new identity, but she can't work undercover anymore. She needed a break; she saw too much, she said she needed to heal herself. She wants kids of her own and said she just couldn't do this anymore knowing what she does. So…"

"So what?"

"So, are you going back to work out there somewhere Lizzie? What are your plans next? We know you have no desire to run the companies. We know you …well, Bao and I are concerned. We both know you have an interest in this kind of thing and the stomach for dealing with it. Yeah, I remember you wanted to be in on things in Sao Paulo when Julia and the twins were kidnapped. Your dad would have none of it. You handled the ladies perfectly after what they had been through…and Julia told us about Highland. I know the settings in those third-world countries. I'm sure you are sick of it too."

Lizzie laughed nervously and put her thumb on her chin. "Are you asking if I would take her spot? I've never done undercover work. I do know what to look for, though if they are trafficking, we are trained to spot abuse. I can handle myself and …I, yes, I think I could do this. I know more about poison arrows than guns though…"

This time both Bao and Chuck laugh, thinking that she is kidding about the poison arrows.

Chuck continued, "You won't be carrying a gun. But we can teach you some surprisingly good self-defense, just in case. I am not saying it is not dangerous. It is. These people kill people. They torture people. You will be wired sometimes, particularly when we think we are getting close to our objective. You speak Spanish, Cambodian, and a fair bit of Chinese now, I understand, after working in the city, let alone what you picked up in Africa… What? Swahili? We have kids being stolen from many countries and used here and sadly, even our own kids. We are watching a group in Tlaxcala and in Phoenix that are trading Native Americans as illegal workers and sex slaves. Over five hundred native American children and women have disappeared in the last two years. No one seems to care. The feds consider it the problem with the tribes. Where would they get the power to take these cartels down? They can't. We can."

"We? Bao, are you part of this too?"

"Yes, since after Sao Paulo. Julia, your parents, Chuck. They had the assets and could do things the government couldn't or wouldn't. We all decided this would make a difference. Chuck had a team of men and women out of the military that wanted in and were willing to give their lives to it. None of them have families or children. That's the rule. We found it too hard for the guys who had kids to keep their stuff together when they saw what was being done to these babies. Some of the girls are barely out of the toddler stage. We are a secret service, when and where it is needed. Julia wanted to call us God's Warriors. The unit is called 'Lakeside'. Your dad, Chuck, and I came up with it, sitting by the lake one night. I think John and I needed to deal with our own demons about what happened on our own lake so many years ago. He never forgave himself. This was a way of paying penance, I guess."

"You never told me. They never told me...why?"

"Lizzie," said Bao, "Your parents hoped that you would marry, have children, save the world, enjoy what they left you. You had all the tools, they thought. They thought you had seen enough hurt, enough death and pain early in your life already. Chuck and I know some kinds of pain never go away; you just have to find a way to kill off the demons, to keep your sanity."

They all sat there for a while looking out at the bay. Seals jumping up on the rocks, barking orders at each other. Each in their own world for a while. Chuck excused himself to make a call to file his return flight plan. Fog was coming in, out in the Monterey Bay.

While Chuck was doing that, Bao put a blank envelope in front of Lizzie. "Open it."

Lizzie was looking at a piece of a newspaper article, a photo of a car in a river, a photo of a young Hispanic man taken off a faked passport. It was the Bolder Times a week ago.

"That's a worker at the Pub I used to go to in Bolder. I wonder what happened to him? Rough crowd, I guess," her eyebrows raised.

"I'm pretty sure I know what happened, Lizzie. Just wonder why?" said Bao.

Lizzie looked outside towards the bay. When she turned back to look at Bao, she ripped the paper up in pieces and put them in her coffee cup. She looked back at Bao with that smile he and Cookie had recently experienced. He didn't ask her again about it.

"Will I get to kill anyone?"

"Maybe," he said. "Most likely. You may have too."

Lizzie smiled. Bao knew that smile. And it sometimes frightened him.

Chuck was right. She had changed. Or had they just not noticed who she was from the very beginning?

About the Author

Suzy Carlile lives in Southern Oregon, east of the Cascades, where storytelling and history abound, but when it used to get too cold before Covid struck, she used to travel to places like Cambodia, Africa, Mexico, and yes, of course, California. Stories are to be found anywhere, especially in your own backyard. Her husband, Rod, has a great sense of humor and asks who she may have killed off on days she is writing Lizzie's tales. Border Collie, Callie, and Toby-tabby cat are her great assistant assassins. More Lizzie and Sandy Curly Fox tales to come. Maybe together, maybe not. They were fun to play with.

Although this is a work of fiction there were four drownings and one unexplained dead body found not far from a women's shelter, in her hometown one summer, and then she heard in the news the next summer about more unusual drownings in several other towns around the state…that's when one's imagination starts to wander. What if?

Made in the USA
Las Vegas, NV
10 December 2022

61675765R00106